WARPATH

The cowboy spun around and Spur's old .44 slammed down on his head, jolting him to the barn floor. Spur tied the guard's feet with his own gun belt, then tied his hands behind him with his handkerchief.

Spur knew he had to work faster now. He found a three-tined pitchfork and stabbed it into the hay. Half way around he hit something hard. Two minutes later he had forked enough hay away so he could see the army rifle boxes.

Inside were six brand-new, army-ready Spencer repeating rifles. The kind of weapons young bucks would kill for. Had killed for. The Secret Service Agent counted the boxes. Twenty of them. All full. That meant a hundred-and-twenty rifles. Enough to start a full-scale Indian rebellion!

Also in the SPUR Series:

SPUR #22

DAKOTA DOXY

Dirk Fletcher

LEISURE BOOKS ❧ NEW YORK CITY

A LEISURE BOOK

Published by

Dorchester Publishing Co., Inc.
6 East 39th Street
New York, New York 10016

Printed in the United States of America

DAKOTA DOXY

1

The scorpion edged forward on its four pair of thin legs, its sensory organs picking up the unusual scent of moisture in this dry time. It moved up the blue cloth that covered the man's arm, went over his shoulder and touched the wetness cautiously. Its long pointed stinger tail curved gracefully over its back ready to jolt down and sting any small prey that it could capture for food.

For a moment the three-inch long scorpion hesitated, then it sent out its long feelers with their strong pincers on the end and caught at the heart of the wetness. The gentle probing brought a reaction, a sudden movement by the large man animal. For a few seconds the male scorpion was absolutely still as it sensed danger. The form the scorpion sat on shivered, then moved, and the large spider-like creature lost its hold on the fabric and tumbled a foot onto the chest of the man thing it had found lying in the alley.

The man groaned.

He lifted one hand to his head, then his pale green eyes blinked and opened staring hard into the night's blackness.

There was no moon.

The man winced, groaned again as he tried to move his left arm. He stared down at the creature on his chest.

His right hand moved so fast the scorpion had no defense. The hard fingers flicked the creature off his chest into the dirt where it scuttered for the edge of the garbage barrel next to the back of a store.

"A damn predacious arthropod of the order of Scorpionida," he mumbled, not sure where the words came from or why he said them.

He winced and then bleated in pain as he started to sit up.

Automatically he reached for his six-gun in tied down leather at his right thigh.

The holster was empty.

When he turned his head quickly, a hundred thousand of the white man's flies buzzed as if they were making honey and heading for the hive or to a bee tree inside his skull. Slowly the buzzing stopped.

He could sit up now. He stared at the alley where he found himself. What was he doing here?

When he found no answer, he looked down at his left shoulder. Even in the dimness of the dark alley, he could see the blood where it had seeped from the wound that must be under his blue shirt.

"Got myself shot," he whispered. The voice he heard was not familiar. For a moment he scowled as he thought it over.

The simple truth was he had no idea why he was in this alley. He did not know who had shot him or why. But the most grating truth of all came with the sudden understanding that he also did not have the faintest notion who he was.

He checked for a wallet or purse. He carried none in his pants. Franctically he felt in his shirt pocket. There was only one item there, a torn off piece of paper from a cheap school tablet that said:

"Minot, Dakota Territory. Be there Tuesday."

A shot boomed in the street beyond the store. Angry voices pleaded. A new deeper voice seemed to intervene, and then there was quiet for a moment.

The deep voice came again, clear through the night air.

"We find the sonofabitch or none of you men ever work for us again, you understand that, you half-broke, steer dumb assholes? Now we keep looking until we find the bastard if it takes all night, if it takes all week!"

They were hunting someone. Hired guns hunting someone to kill him. Slowly the man sitting in the dirt realized he could be the man they were hunting. He was shot, he wasn't sure it *wasn't him*. So he had to move.

Slowly he got on his hands and knees, and holding his left arm tightly against his chest, he crawled up the garbage barrel lifting and pulling with his right hand until he could stand.

Once on his feet it was simpler. His legs were fine, felt strong. He was not heavy, fat or old.

He had a fighting chance!

The wounded man started at a fast walk, then a slow trot down the alley away from the brightest lights. He realized at once that whatever or whoever he was, he was not a coward, or a man to give up easily. And he also was not stupid: he had no weapon so he couldn't fight a group of armed men.

"Run away and live to fight another day." He breathed the words somebody long dead had coined.

When he came to the intersecting street, he paused against the clapboard side of a building which could have been a small two story hotel. Nobody was on the street. A buggy rattled past on the dirt surface of the cross street half a block down, then all was silent.

A shot sounded the other way down the cross street.

He walked carefully, stepping down from the boardwalk into the dust of the street, across the ten yards of space to the boardwalk on the other side and back into the darkness of an alley.

He leaned against the rough bricks of the building next to the alley and looked back down the street he had just crossed.

It was typical for a small Western town. This could be Minot, Dakota Territory. He knew where it was, not much more than fifty miles from the Canadian border. A long two days ride on a good horse.

The wounded man frowned, his green eyes clouding with wonder. He was learning something about himself. He knew horses, he must be able to use a six-gun, and he knew where Minot was in the Dakota Territory.

Not a damn lot to go on when a gang of gunmen were hunting for his hide. But it was a small start.

He turned and jogged into the darkness. The stores on the right side petered out and soon he was in an alley that ran between occasional houses.

To the left he could see the outlines of a big barn, and the smell of horses came to him plainly. He turned that way without knowing why. Cautiously he tried to reason it out. Instinct for survival? Programmed understanding and knowledge? He had no idea. He didn't even know how he came up with such words. Was he an educated man, a cowboy, or maybe an outlaw?

He ran now, pumping his right arm, keeping his left arm tightly against his chest, his hand gripping his shirt to steady it.

One coal oil lantern still burned at the double wide doors of the livery. Over the door he saw the lettering: "Minot Livery Stables, W.W. Wilson, prop."

The man scowled at the light, then using some small shrubs and trees along the edge of the street, managed to get almost to the door before he had to step into the light. He took three long strides and was through the door and out of the wick's glow.

The smells and animals sounds in the barn were familiar. The man put that down in his memory about who he was. His eyes glanced around, saw a young man sleeping on a blanket stretched out in an empty stall. He roused the lad with his boot.

"Wasn't sleeping, Mr. Wilson!" the boy said jolting to a sitting position in one reflexive burst.

"I'm not Wilson. You got a horse I can rent?"

The lad stood, stared at him a minute, then motioned toward the second lantern that hung outside a shed-like office.

The man went with the boy who brought the lantern off the nail and passed it close to his visitor's face.

"Yep, you're the one. Damn but you blasted those

bastard Diamond D riders! They had it coming. Course Harry ain't gonna stop until he finds you and ventilates your hide to a fair thee well." He stopped.

"Christ, I see he already started." For a moment he frowned and shook his head. "I can't help you much. For damn sure I can't rent you a horse. Harry would cut my balls off and laugh as I screamed. He's a wild sonofabitch."

The stable hand motioned the man inside the shack.

"I can stop the bleeding and wrap up that shoulder some. That way you won't bleed to death. Inside and quick. Harry sent two of his riders here ten minutes ago. They'll be checking back every fifteen minutes or so. Harry said he had to have your scalp for what you did to his brother, Edward."

They stepped into the shed, which was a small office with a bunk on one side. The lad brought out a pint of whiskey and some clean clothes from a small tin box, then cut away part of the blood-stained shirt.

"Clean hole," he said nodding. "Course it didn't come out. Must have been half spent when it hit you. Ricochet maybe. That slug has to come out in three days, or you're in damn big trouble. My old man is a doctor back in St. Louis." He swabbed at the small purple bullet hole a moment.

"Oh, I'm Ned, Ned Burton. I'm seventeen and I'm aiming to be a lawman someday. If I can learn to hit anything with a .44."

He watched as the man winced when he sopped the whiskey over the wound.

"Don't know why, exactly, but whiskey or alcohol

makes a wound heal better. Stops the infection somehow." He put a pad of the clean cloth over the wound and bound it in place with white sticky adhesive tape. Then he wrapped long strips of the cloth around the man's wound, under his arm and over his other shoulder and back to hold the bandage tightly.

Ned stepped back and grinned.

"There, you're ready to fight again. Not as good as new, but better. I . . . I really think what you did was the right thing. Nobody else in town will stand up to the Diamond D riders, no matter what they do. I admire that you did it."

He scuffed his feet on the floor. Ned wore no gun. He looked nervous, glancing at the door.

"Hate to do it, but you better get away from here. Harry and his men will be back soon. They counted my rent horses last time. I surely do think you done the right thing. Lord knows Virgin is so grateful she can't even replay. I mean, look what they were doing to her and right there on Main Street in daylight!

"Ed had it coming, far as I'm concerned, and he was the one who started it, and who jumped up first when you challenged the four of them."

"Virgin?" the man asked.

"Yeah, the woman, her name is Virgin. Didn't you even know that?"

"Guess I didn't. I thank you for the patch up." He walked out the door toward the front of the Livery.

"I better be moving so I don't get you in any trouble, Ned. Thanks again for the medical work. I appreciate it. I'll make it up to you."

"No account to do that, sir. I just wanted to help. Be careful. I . . . I never seen one man up against three guns that way. You killed that one guy and wounded the other one. Everybody says the slug that hit you came from the side, from a fourth gunman. I hope you're all right."

"I'll make it, Ned."

"Best bet for you would be the brush down along the river. Lots of thick stuff down there. Crawl into the bramble patches. Not even the Diamond D men will crash into there."

"Thanks, kid. Thanks." The man walked through the splash of light quickly and once in the darkness spotted the blacker line of trees near the Souris River. He frowned. How did he know the name of the river?

He must have been coming here for a purpose. What was it? At least he was remembering a little. But he needed a whole lot more before he could figure out what was going on.

The tall man with sideburns down to his jaw line walked swiftly now toward the river. It was less than two hundred yards behind the livery.

Halfway there he heard someone behind him. Footsteps. Someone was running. He crouched in the darkness to make himself a smaller target. Perhaps he could trip the person, strangle him with bare hands.

With a reflexive action he tried to draw his six-gun. There was no iron there.

The steps came closer, then they slowed and he could see a form moving toward him against the back lighting of the town's lanterns.

When the figure was six feet away, he rose up in a rush and lunged at the person.

"No. I won't hurt you. I'm here to help."

It was a woman's voice, small, frightened, but somehow at the same time, stern and knowing.

"You've just been in the livery and got bandaged. I'm here to help you, but I couldn't involve Ned."

He had stopped as soon as he heard her voice. Now he watched as the woman came toward him. In the darkness he saw only that she wore a dress and a shawl over her shoulders. Her hair was dark but he could not make out her features.

"I'm the woman you saved from being raped on the street this afternoon. Now it's my turn to help you. If I don't, Harry Renshew and his gang of gunmen will run you to ground and shoot you fifty times."

She paused. "You're wounded, and you're being hunted by evil men with no morals who will surely kill you. I don't even know your name, but I hope you're not too proud to take help from me. My name is Virgin, I'm a whore and you saved my life this afternoon. Now it's my turn to help you."

The man felt the dizziness come again. It had been coming and going as he walked. He had no idea how much blood he had lost. The lady was right. He could use some help. Maybe then she would explain enough to him so he could figure out who he was, and why he was in Minot way up here in the northern part of the territory.

He moved a step closer.

She put out her hand and slowly he let her put it around his waist as he put his arm over her shoulder.

"You don't even know who I am."

"I know all I have to. You helped me, now I have a chance to return the favor."

"Like saving my life?"

"Yes, the way you saved me today."

They walked silently, and he saw that they were in the high plains grasslands just behind the town. She was taking him the long way around to the other side of town.

Twice they stopped and sat on the grass when his steps became so slow that she was afraid he would fall.

"You need to rest," she told him. "I can't let you pass out, because if you do, I can't carry you."

After one more stop they reached the destination. It was a small house two full blocks from any other building at the edge of town. It was not on any trail and looked unused.

She looked around in the darkness, then pushed open the back door and they walked inside. The place did not smell musty and unused although that was how it seemed from the outside.

Instead it smelled of alcohol and blood that tinged the delicious odor of a beef stew that bubbled slowly on the wood-burning kitchen stove.

She lit a candle in the bedroom. He saw that she had nailed blankets over the window and kept the door closed.

"No one must know we're here," she said. For the first time she turned so he could see her face. One of her eyes were swollen shut. There was a gash on her left cheek that she had patched together and bandaged. Her stark black hair looked softer now. She had combed it the best she could since that afternoon.

She was the same woman he remembered in bits and flashes. Yes! She had been flat on her back on the boardwalk and three cowboys were hooting and laughing as they stripped her clothes off her. One had tied her hands above her head to spikes driven into the boardwalk.

They hooted and laughed and then the scene flashed away and he could remember no more.

"Lay down, I'll bring you some supper. You need rest and food and a digger to get that bullet out of your shoulder."

"The riders won't find us here?" he asked.

"Not unless they break into every house in town. Not even the Diamond D has that kind of power yet in Minot. They own the sheriff, but not everyone agrees with what they do."

A moment later she brought in a bowl of stew, and a cup of hot coffee, with a two-inch slice of fresh baked bread. She set it in front of him and he realized he was hungry. He couldn't remember when he had eaten last.

When the bowl of stew was empty, she brought another with more bread and this time a jar of strawberry jam and more coffee. By the time the bowl was empty this time, his eyes sagged and closed. She took away the dishes and when she came back he was sleeping.

She put one hand to his forehead. It was warm but not feverish. She nodded in thanks. Virgin slumped in a rocking chair where she could watch him. The next few hours would be important. He looked strong, but a bullet in a man can do strange things to his state of health.

Virgin was a small, finely honed woman, barely five feet two, with a slender waist and surprisingly large breasts. She put a cold cloth on her eye, wetting it frequently, and little by little the swelling came down. There was nothing she could do about the gash on her cheek.

It had been made by a knife while she was still standing. She refused to think about the attack. She had fought them. The ugly part had been that it happened in public. Men had used her body in every way possible and some tried the impossible.

But never in public. Never on a town's main street in daylight. Never for spite and out of anger and by force!

She blinked back tears. She cried as any woman cried. She bled and sorrowed and agonized as any other female.

But some men could never understand that. To them she was simply a whore for their pleasure; drunk or sober, upstairs or on the boardwalk it made no difference to them.

She dried her tears and replaced the cold cloth on the man's forehead. She liked the reddish brown color of his thick hair. He mumbled and pushed the cloth away in his sleep. She returned it and held it there. The bullet had to come out. She had examined the wound. There was no exit mark. That was bad.

Virgin knew she would have to go for Frances in the morning. There was a chance her house was being watched by Renshew or his men. It was a risk she had to take.

Otherwise this beautiful man who had saved her life would die.

At midnight he woke, mumbled something and looked at her in surprise. Evidently it took him a few seconds to remember where he was and what had happened.

"Aren't you going to sleep?" he asked.

"I'll nap in the chair."

"Plenty of room in the bed . . . Don't worry, I won't attack you. I'm feeling the loss of blood."

He moved over in the double bed and she lay down beside him. Both were fully clothed. She had pulled a light blanket up over him and now snuggled it around her. He lay on his back and looked at her.

"Now isn't that better?" he asked softly.

"Yes, I am tired. I . . . I don't even know your name."

He paused. "I don't think it's a good idea for you to know that right now. In a few days. Let's see what happens. Is that all right?"

"Yes," she hesitated, eyebrows knitted in the half light of the candle. "But what should I call you?"

"George. I'll be George for a while."

"Good night, George," she said.

"Good night, Virgin."

A half hour later he was still wide awake. She had dropped off at once and then had turned on her side and curled against him, her head against his shoulder, her knees bent and touching his hip.

He reached across her and snuffed out the candle.

For another hour the tall man with green eyes, sandy colored hair and full moustache lay on the bed beside Virgin, wondering who he was and again, why he was in Minot. Had he come here for some specific purpose? And was he gunsharp or U.S. Marshal, hero or villain?

He knew little for certain, except that the woman sleeping beside him had probably saved his life tonight. Tomorrow was a different matter. Tomorrow he had to find someone to dig that slug out of his shoulder.

He figured the men looking for him would know his problem, and would be waiting for him at the doctor's office. That was if this little town of five hundred people even had a doctor.

Five hundred people? How did he know that?

Slowly the man drifted into sleep where he dreamed of a gunfight, and a pretty woman spread-eagled on the boardwalk, and a man with a six-gun with a three-inch-diameter barrel about to shoot him from two feet away without a chance in hell of missing!

2

A soft humming battered at his consciousness. He started to turn over, but the movement sent a jolt of pain through his shoulder and he settled back down, eyes still closed. He was somewhere blissfully wonderful between sleep and wakefulness.

For a moment he realized someone was moving around nearby, but he couldn't open his eyes. Sounds drifted to him but he did his best to ignore them. But when the next assault came, he popped open his eyes at once.

The crisp smell of frying bacon sifted through the doorway into the bedroom, and was followed quickly by the enticing scent of boiling coffee.

He started to sit up from the bed as he always did, but the knifing pain in his shoulder stopped him.

Then he remembered. He had a slug in his shoulder, and it had to come out. He turned, lifted his boots and levered himself to a sitting posture, swung his legs off the bed and stood. He was still fully dressed.

The sandy haired man rubbed his right hand over

21

his stubbled face, and experimented with his left arm. He could raise his hand and forearm by holding his shoulder absolutely still. Any movement of his upper arm or shoulder sent stabbing needles of pain into his upper chest. Gingerly he took a step toward the door.

His right hand went to his holster, and only then did he remember that he could not remember. Everything was as blank as a white snow bank beyond late yesterday afternoon.

He knew a little about himself but not a hell of a lot. He needed to find out a great deal more if he were to stay alive. His best and closest source was the woman who had rescued him and shared her bed with him.

In the other half of the small house that served as living room and kitchen, he found Virgin. She had brushed her long dark hair until it shone, and tied it with a string to form a cascading pony tail half way down her back. He had noticed little about her last night. Now he saw that she was maybe twenty-one or two, with a pretty face and dark eyes under full brows and a small, cupid mouth and a dimple on her right cheek. She wore a fresh white blouse and a divided blue skirt.

"Good morning," he said.

"Good morning, George," she replied without looking at him. She picked up a stoneware white china plate. "Breakfast is ready."

He sat down and she put in front of him the plate filled with four eggs sunnyside up, a half a plate of hash brown potatoes, two slices of thick toast and six slices of crisp bacon. A steaming cup of coffee sat beside the plate.

"You didn't have to go to all this trouble."

She looked at him with faint disapproval.

"George, it's been years since anyone gave a damn about me, let along got into a fist fight. And nobody ever took up gunplay over me. My father booted me out of the house when I was fourteen because he caught me and a neighbor boy fooling around with our clothes off. We both were just as curious as hell, but nothing happened. We hardly touched each other. Since then, I've been on my own."

She laughed softly and sat down across from him at a second plate where she had started eating.

"Besides, don't you know the old Chinese custom? In China, if you save a person's life, you become their slave for life. I just became Chinese, so I'm bound to do everything for you that I can. Somehow dead just has never held any great appeal to me."

He watched her a moment, saw a sly smile begin to grow around the right side of her face where there was no bandage. Her eye was almost back to normal with the swelling down.

"Chinese, eh? I'll call you Soo Lame Duk."

They both laughed and went on eating. She sighed and sat back.

"I haven't had a good laugh like that for months." She stood and reached for a jacket. "Right now I've got to slip over to a lady friend of mine and see if Frances can come here. That lead must come out of your shoulder."

"Will the Diamond D riders be watching her place?"

"I doubt it this early. They were probably up most of the night looking for you. It's a chance we have to take."

She buttoned her coat and looked over at her benefactor.

"You stay put. There's more coffee. I should be back in half an hour." She put on a hat that almost covered her face. "There's a chance that those same men might see me, but I doubt it. If they do I've got a surprise for them."

She took from the coat pocket a .32 caliber woman's six-gun.

"Is it loaded and can you shoot it?" he asked.

"Yes to both questions. Five rounds and the hammer is on an empty chamber. Oh, I almost forgot." She reached to a high shelf next to the kitchen stove and took down something wrapped in a heavy cloth.

When he opened it he found a well worn Colt .44 of uncertain origin. He checked the action. It was loaded. In the cloth was a box of fifty rounds. He hefted the iron, slid it into his holster and pulled it out. It had a well worn, honest feel.

"Thanks, I feel dressed now. Be careful."

Virgin nodded, flashed a smile and hurried out the door. From the drawn blinds, he watched her walking swiftly down the trail to the street, then toward the houses and town. He lost her behind the first house and went back to the last of his breakfast. Then he stacked the dishes on the counter with the dish pan and put on water to heat on the back of the stove. It had no built in boiler.

Before the water got hot, he saw Virgin coming back. Half a block behind her walked another woman, a black who stood straight and tall, with a scarf tied around her head and a small black bag in her hand.

He automatically watched both sides, but saw no one following them. He ran to the bedroom window where he had a better view and carefully scanned every open area in front of the house toward town but saw no one move. Maybe they had been lucky.

When he heard both women come into the house,

he left the window and walked into the small living room. He carried his left arm against his chest.

"Take off your shirt," Frances said. "We have maybe ten minutes." She handed him a pint of whiskey. "Drink, it may help. But sit down at the table where you won't fall down if you pass out. It's gonna hurt plenty bad."

"I've done this before," the man said. He frowned as he said it. He could not remember even being shot at before. He sat at the table. Frances tied a long belt around him pinning his back to the chair. She laid his left arm on the table and stared at the small blue hole which had puckered slightly and now showed redness for an inch around it.

"I appreciate your doing this," the man said.

She nodded. "Drink and shut up," Frances said grinning. She opened the black bag but wouldn't let him see inside. He took another long pull on the whiskey, coughed, then drank again.

"Don't watch," Francis commanded. "Virgin, you stand beside him and don't let him fall off the chair."

Without warning the long, thin probe slid into his flesh. He gagged down a scream, then gritted his teeth staring at a spot on the unpainted far wall until his eyes clouded and he closed them.

A groan seeped from his lips as the steel probe worked deeper into the fleshy part of his shoulder.

Frances sloshed some of the whiskey over the bullet hole and he screamed. The pain was like a white hot iron rod driving itself slowly into his shoulder, searing the flesh, burning a hole as it went. He felt as if he might throw up, then the fire burned hotter and hotter and a million stars burst in back of his eyes and a cooling, soothing cascade of a mountain stream flooded over him offering a cool alternative to the white hot poker.

His head lolled forward as the man passed out.

"Hold his head!" Frances snapped. "Now we can work before he comes to."

Virgin caught his chin and lifted it out of the way of the left shoulder.

The tall, black woman licked her lips in concentration as she worked with the probe.

"Yes, Lord. I've found it. So deep." She pushed another probe into the small wound and worked for two minutes.

"Making progress. Another inch or so." At last she pushed and lifted and the lead slug edged out of the hole. She grabbed it with her fingers and pulled it free. At once she poured whiskey over the wound, took a fresh compress from her bag and taped it in place to stop the gush of blood. Then she put a thin strip of bandage over the compress, around his shoulder and arm to hold the bandage in place, and stepped back.

Together they unfastened him from the chair and lifted him and dragged him into the bedroom and lay him on the bed.

"Watch him for at least twenty-four hours. Don't let that shoulder bleed."

"Yes, Frances. I'll watch him good."

The touch of a smile softened her stern black face. "Child, I know you will." She wiped perspiration from her forehead. "After yesterday . . . I worried most of the night. You all right, child? They hurt you?"

"Frances, I'm fine, just banged up a little. We've both seen lots worse. But if he hadn't come along..."

"We don't talk about that, Virgin. You watch him. He's a good man. I got me a feeling."

"I will. Now you be careful about getting back

into town. Better go out the back door and down to the river for a ways and . . ."

Virgin laughed. Then Frances joined her.

"Reckon I know about what to do, child." Frances held out her arms and the women hugged each other. Then without a word, Frances put on her coat, washed off the probes in the water boiling on the stove and hurried out the back door.

Virgin locked and bolted the door, did the same to the front, then took a double barreled shotgun from the small closet and put shells in both slots and snapped the breach closed. She was ready if anyone came.

An hour later, the man who called himself George woke up with a short scream and a long grinding groan. Virgin, who had been watching the town from behind the blind on the kitchen window, hurried in to him.

His face was white with the pain, but he forced a smile.

"No worse than a bad cold, I'll be out of here in an hour or two."

"You'll do no such thing. You need rest and good food."

He listened for a moment.

"A rider's coming. You expecting company?"

"Not friendly."

He swung out of the bed and put his boots on the floor. "He's riding to the back door. Kitchen."

The man moved slowly to the kitchen over Virgin's protests. He held the six-gun in his right hand. In the kitchen he saw the shotgun and motioned for her to hand it to him. George sat in a chair that faced the back door, the shotgun over his knees pointed at the door. He was still without a shirt and the chill of the early morning brought goose bumps to his flesh.

Someone outside pounded on the kitchen door.

"Open up!" a gruff man's voice demanded.

George shook his head and held a finger across his lips.

A minute later a boot landed against the door about where the door handle was. The door lock popped off but the bolt above held the door closed. Two more kicks and the bolt screw holders tore loose and the door slammed inward.

A man charged into the room reaching for a gun in his leather.

"Freeze, cousin, or I'll blow you in half!" George bellowed before the draw could be completed.

The gunman from outside was three inches under six feet, broad from good food and wearing range clothes. He stopped at once, staring at the twin shotgun muzzles.

"What the hell is the scattergun for?" the invader asked.

"That's what we greet everyone with who kicks in our door," George said softly yet with a deadly tone that left the man both worried and cautious.

"Damn, maybe I have the wrong house." He appeared flustered and sheepish. "Looks like I made me one hell of a big mistake. Ain't this the Johnson place?"

"No, and you'll pay for the door!" Virgin shouted at him.

He ducked and winced. "Yes, ma'am. Shore will. Guess I better be goin'." He turned and headed for the door. Then in a quick move he spun grabbing his six-gun and dropped to his knee.

The man with the shotgun pulled both triggers. Twenty-six double-ought pellets each as big as a .32 round slammed from the twin barrels shredding everything in their path.

The way George held the weapon it became an over and under instead of side by side. The upper barrel's slugs tore into the gunman's neck nearly cutting his head from his body. The lower barrel drove its slugs into the Diamond D rider's chest, pulping his heart and lungs and blasting him out the door and down the steps where he sprawled on his back in the dust, dead before he knew what happened.

"My God!" Virgin keened and turned away. The man who knew himself only as George moved to the back door and looked out. A Diamond D branded horse stood at the tie rail. The body might not be found for hours.

"We better get out of here," George said. "You know any real safe place I can hide out for a day or two?"

"Oh, God!" Virgin said again. She stared at the body out the door. He caught her shoulders and turned her away.

"Virgin, we need to leave here. More of them will come. He'll be missed."

"Yes . . . I've never seen a man . . . not blown apart that way . . . Oh, God!"

He talked to her quietly for a few minutes, and at last she unfroze, her eyes returned to normal and she took a deep breath.

"Yes, I know where we can go. If you don't mind living in an old Indian cave. No one knows about it anymore."

It took them ten minutes more to get supplies in a gunny sack, then a pillow-case of food and rolled blankets. George took the shotgun and a box of shells and the six-gun and shells and they went to a small shed at the back of the place where two horses fed in a stall.

George tried to throw a saddle on the first horse and groaned with pain. At last he worked the saddle on the nag with his right hand, and got it cinched up.

They rode away from town, then to the north along the river and into the first large sized valley that quickly turned into a draw, and then into a ridge of sandy cliffs and dry sandstone walls. A quarter of a mile up the draw she turned her horse down a faint track that led to a clump of willow and brush.

He had been thinking about himself. Back there he knew what the gunman was going to try. It had been like shooting fish in a barrel. But he had not hesitated to kill the man. He had done it before he was sure, but as an outlaw or a lawman? He had no idea. He knew now he was not afraid to use his weapons, and he was good with them. He'd target-practice with the pistol to sight it in, learn just where it fired at twenty feet. His last .44 had been a little high and to the right. He frowned. His last .44? When was that?

She pulled her horse to a stop in the brush and dismounted.

"We walk from here. It's too steep to ride. The horses can make it. If we leave them here it's a dead give-away."

She led the way into a narrow gorge that had sandstone cliffs thirty feet high. There was barely room for the horses to walk through. On the far side the way went up a steep slope that had the sure-footed animals slipping and sliding.

Nothing but sandstone cliffs were all around them. They went across a short flat stretch, then down for a hundred yards along a gentle slope to a tiny valley no more than twenty yards in diameter.

A thin stain of water ran through the center.

At the far side a blush of green showed more willow and a few maple and ash. Virgin tied her horse there and picked up the heaviest sack of supplies.

"Almost there. Can you get down?"

He did and they went through the trees to a sandstone wall. They had to push the growth out to get past, but twenty feet ahead they found an opening in the wall. It was the mouth of a cave that led slightly upward into the heart of the mountain.

It was twenty feet to the top of the cavern, and fifty feet into it he saw a bright shaft of sunlight.

A chimney opened to the sky at that point. Grass and flowers grew around the sunny spot that was fed by a spring that bubbled out of rocks on the far side. The cave continued on the other side of the open spot and ten feet inside the cave Virgin put down the sack.

"Home sweet home. What do you think?"

"Nothing could be safer. Water, some wood, I can get all we need. And no one will ever find us here."

She put the blankets down in the sunshine to form a bed.

"Now, you lay down and have a nap. You need rest and good food, and as your nurse I intend to see that you get them."

He sat down on the pad of blankets, then stretched out in the sun favoring his left shoulder. It did feel good to relax for a minute. The questions came again. He called to her and she came out with an apple and told him to eat it.

"Sit down, Virgin. There are some answers I need, and you can help me."

"Yes, George, of course." She sat beside him.

"First, tell me all you know about the Diamond D.

Who owns it, what he's like. How the outfit works, how it is thought of in town, everything."

"Oh, I figured you knew that. But then somebody said you just got off the stage at noon yesterday. Didn't give you much time, I guess.

"All right. The Diamond D is owned by Tom Renshew. He came here twenty years ago, put together some land, got homesteads when the law went through. The word is he got homesteads for about a dozen of his hands as well and all proved up on them and turned them over to Tom.

"Anyway, he owns a big chunk of land north and west of town, and controls both sides of the Souris River for twenty miles upstream. His plan is to control every water source, and then no other rancher can come into the area."

"Then he can use the range between all the water sources like it's his own, right?"

"Yes. You do know about ranches." She frowned slightly and went on. "He has two sons, Edward and Harry. You shot Edward who was trying to rape me out there on the boardwalk. He was drunk and he started it. Dragged me out there and had his helpers hold me down . . .

"The Diamond D is virtually the only functioning ranch in the area. Others have tried, but they go broke, or a barn burns down, or rustlers get their cattle, or an Indian raid burns them out and kills everyone in the operation."

He held up his hand. "Indians? I thought this was Yanktonai country. They've been peaceful for the past ten years."

"Supposedly. But from what I hear, it's some of the young bucks who get restless and go on raids for new horses and maybe a white wife. Nobody has ever tried to get back in there where their main camp is. The army says it's too busy."

"Is this Renshew a fair man?"

Virgin laughed, touched the bandage on her cheek. "He doesn't know what the word means. He's a skunk and has the whole county in his hip pocket. Anything he wants done, gets done. Anyone he wants elected, gets elected. The mayor said they should change the name of the county to Renshew County. The next day Ed Renshew came to town, called the mayor out and shot him dead. Nobody makes jokes about the Renshews anymore.

"I better get some food ready. I'm hungry and I know you should be eating. It's almost noontime."

He moved to the cave and sat on a blanket and watched her. She made a small fire in an ages-old fire ring circled with blackened rocks that wouldn't explode when they heated up. The blaze was a cooking fire that she let burn down to glowing coals.

"What about the county sheriff?" he asked.

"Renshew owns him too. He tends to legal matters and doesn't bother much with criminal law, especially if it involves Renshew, his ranch, or about half of the business firms in town that Renshew owns and runs."

"Sounds like a great little kingdom Renshew has here," he said frowning.

"You say that downtown and you're a dead man the next day," Virgin said. "Why do you suppose nobody came to help me when Ed Renshew wanted to have his way with me on the boardwalk in broad daylight?"

She worked on boiling some potatoes and fixing some ground beef to fry. At last she looked up.

"Could I ask you a question?" He nodded. "Just who are you and why are you here in Minot?"

He sat up and frowned. "Virgin, I can't tell you

that. I wish I could. Ever since I woke up in that alley last night I haven't known who I am or why I'm in town. I can't remember a thing that happened to me before I went to the livery and then met you outside. That's my first job, Virgin. I've got to find out whom I am and just what the hell I'm doing in Dakota Territory.''

3

Tom Renshew thundered his fist down on the massive oak kitchen table in the big house at the Diamond D Ranch five miles out from Minot. His face flushed crimson as he screamed at his son and foreman. He had been on his feet for more than twenty-four hours and the strain was plain.

"Find the bastard and castrate him, then cut his dick off and then gouge his damned eyes out! I'll make him suffer for a week and then I'll chop him up a chunk at a time until the shithead dies! Do I make myself clear?"

Renshew was not a big man at two inches under six feet, but he was sturdy, strongly built with rich black hair and dark brows. Now his fist slammed onto the heavy oak table again making the coffee cups bounce.

"Search every house in town if you have to. The fucking bastard killed Edward, and now he blew Zach's head off with a shotgun. I want the asshole more than anything in my life! I want him now! Take the town apart. I'm riding in shortly to have

35

wanted posters put up.

"I'll give five thousand dollars in gold coins to the man who brings me this son-of-a-bitch alive!"

"Five thousand!" Harry Renshew, Tom's only surviving child, said softly. "Christ, Dad, that's a lot of money. That's more than they had for Billy the Kid."

Tom ignored him as he had for most of the past twenty years. All of his concentration, his teaching, his love had been heaped on Edward, and now Edward was dead. Cut down by some bastard with a fast gun. Tom realized that he'd have to start training Harry to take over the ranch.

The boy was a Renshew so he was smart enough, and he must have picked up a lot just living on the ranch. Maybe he was better equipped to do the job than Ed had been. Tom drank from the coffee cup and slammed it down on the sturdy table. The cup broke and splattered coffee over the cloth.

The man who controlled over 250,000 acres of prime grazing land north along the Souris River turned to his foreman.

"Jed, I want you to pull in every man we have. Be sure each rider has a pistol and a rifle. If we don't have enough I'll get more. Then I want you to take a chuck wagon and camp at the edge of town on the river and I want every man-Jack of us to be on patrol in that damned little town.

"The minute that murdering bastard pokes his head up for air, we nail his ass. But I want him *alive!* Then we start taking him apart, his balls come off first and I get to castrate the fucker. You got that straight?"

"Yes sir, Mr. Renshew. I'll split the crew, half on nights and half days, twelve hour shifts. We'll track him down."

"How man men can you scrape up, Jed?"

"Right now we got about thirty hands. I was planning that trail drive last of next week."

"Cancel the drive. Put twenty men on at night, and ten during the day. I want every goddamned man, woman and child in town to know that if this no-name bastard gets helped by any of them, they'll be tarred and feathered and run out of town."

"Yes sir, Mr. Renshew."

"Don't stand there, Jedediah, get your ass moving. Send everyone into town that you can right now."

"Most of the men been up all night, sir."

"So what? So have you and I. Get them up and get them moving, now!"

Jed nodded and ducked out of the big kitchen. It was a ranch style cookery, with three of the largest kitchen ranges Renshew could find along one wall. There were cupboards, pantries, bins for hundred pound sacks of flour, sugar and potatoes. His cooks had served a formal dinner for more than fifty people from this kitchen. But now he saw none of it, he had blood in his eyes and it wouldn't clear until Ed's killer was caught, punished, tortured, made to understand the enormity of his crime and then slowly killed.

Tom stared at his second son, now his only heir.

"Harry, I want you on the day shift, I'll take the night. First I need to get some supplies and more rounds for my rifle. We'll find the shitty bastard killer, you can be on that. So move, Harry. Ride with Jed. Get those men moving and tell them about the reward."

"Dad, that's wages for a cowhand for over fourteen years!"

"I can afford it. I want every drifter, every gunsharp, every bounty hunter in the territory gunning for that damned killer."

Harry caught his hat from the table, finished his coffee and went out to the corral. He had had less than two hours sleep last night. They had watched every saloon in town. The man simply had not surfaced.

Tom watched his son leave the house. The boy had a lot to learn. He was not tough enough. Edward had been mean and hard, the kind of man needed to run a spread this size. A man who could take what he wanted, what he needed and hold it. Tom was not at all certain that Harry could do that, not yet. He was only twenty-four, lots of time to train him the right way. They would start that special training just as soon as this murderer was caught.

Tom pulled new cup from a rack and filled it with coffee, stirred in two spoons full of sugar and sipped at the hot brew. He had been over twenty years building up this spread. He had it set to last for two hundred years, if his sons could keep it together. Now it was up to Harry.

He had concentrated in gathering land north of the small town, along the river which provided the water the stock needed. Control the water, you control everything else. And he had it. Every stream and small lake north from Minot for twenty miles was his—either by homestead, deed or by right—by occupying it and chasing anyone off who tried to squat on it.

The system had worked. Now he had a twenty mile stretch of the river locked in, and he controlled the land for ten miles on each side of the Souris River, giving him about four hundred sections of land. His was by far the biggest ranch in the territory.

And he intended to keep it that way.

No fast gun was going to come into his country and take it away. The man had already hurt him more than Tom Renshew wanted to admit. But soon the bastard killer would pay. Ed's killer would pay with so much pain and agony that he would scream and plead and beg to be killed long before the fucking shitter finally died.

It would be a good object lesson for Harry, toughen him up a little. The boy had to become a man!

Tom bellowed for his cook. The small Chinese man with a long pigtail down his back ran in quickly, bowed and waited.

"Three eggs, six patties of sausage, toast, jam and coffee, and make it snappy. I've got to go into town. Move, you slant-eyed little foreigner!"

Ling rushed toward the range and furiously began cooking the master's breakfast.

When Tom Renshew rode into town an hour later, the good citizens of Minot felt more kindly toward him than they had in years. He had suffered a loss. That in itself was unusual for a Renshew. But this was a son and heir. Most people knew how deeply that wounded a man.

He rode directly to the newspaper office and printing shop and screamed at the printer until he had set up the poster exactly the way Renshew wanted it. He waited in the small plant while the printer ran off a hundred posters. As soon as they were dry he found two small boys and hired them to tack up the wanted posters on every building and post in town.

He didn't even consider paying for the printing. He owned the newspaper and the print shop.

Renshew looked down at the poster and nodded grimly. It should do:

WANTED ALIVE!

The killer who murdered **EDWARD RENSHEW** in Minot. $5,000 Reward!!!!!!!! No name known. MUST BE ALIVE . . .

Description: Male, white, about 30 to 35, six feet two, 200 pounds, sandy hair worn full with chin length sideburns and full moustache. Gun tied low. Armed and Dangerous. For reward contact: Tom Renshew, Minot, Dakota Terr.

A half hour later the town began buzzing with the news of the reward. It was the most reward money any of them could ever remember hearing about, let along having right there in Minot!

Tom Renshew nodded in grim satisfaction. The people in town were reacting the way he thought they would. They might not like him, but they respected his power, and his money. Most men would do anything for money, and to these people, five thousand dollars in hard, cold gold was a fortune.

The damn barber! He had been known to cut a slug out of a cowboy now and then. Renshew stomped down the boardwalk toward the barbershop. Small boys scurried out of his way. Women moved quickly into a shop or store when they saw him coming. He didn't mind. When he noticed it, he enjoyed it.

He banged through the door and stared at Zack Post, who paused in mid clip, then waved the scissors at him.

"Morning, Mr. Renshew. I'm terribly sorry about your loss. My heartfelt sympathies."

"Noted. Thank you. Post, you dug out any lead

lately?"

"Matter of fact I haven't. That man wounded yesterday had a lucky hit, went on through. Haven't seen a bullet hole since then, Mr. Renshew."

"But you do know there's another man around with a slug in him who I'm hunting?"

"I'm aware of that, yes."

"Be unhappy if you did any digging on him. You understand?"

"Indeed I do. Too busy barbering right now, anyway."

"You know where the skunk is hiding?"

"Afraid not, Mr. Renshew, I could use that five thousand dollars much as anybody."

Renshew stared at him sternly, then turned and left.

On the sidewalk, Renshew stared around the town. It wasn't much, but since he owned most of it, he wasn't complaining. He walked into the County Courthouse, a large wooden structure that had been slated to be replaced a dozen times, but each time the taxpayers had not voted the funds.

He went to the lower level of a half basement where the Sheriff's Department was housed. When he opened the door, two women clerks looked up.

"Sheriff Sweet?" he asked.

"He's in his office, Mr. Renshew. Go right on in."

He was going to anyway. Renshew banged the sheriff's office door closed behind him and stared at Lawrence Sweet. The man was a little over thirty years old, five seven, slender with eye glasses and rapidly thinning hair.

He stared up at Renshew over the top of half glasses.

"Sweet, you're the sheriff in this county. Why the hell ain't you out tracking down that killer?"

"Mr. Renshew, you know I don't have much of an enforcement staff. This is an administrative office. We do court work and collect the taxes, and do the assessing . . ."

"I know what the hell you do, Sweet. You know the name of the bastard who killed my son?"

"I'm afraid not."

"Figures. I want you to form up a posse, about twenty men, and start scouring this town for that killer. He can't be far away with a slug in him."

Sweet moved the eyeshade and sat down. He frowned and looked at Renshew. "A posse. I suppose I'm authorized, but I've never done that before."

"Ed has never been murdered before. You can ride a horse?"

"Haven't been on one for two or three years."

"Get the men, deputize them, and remember, the reward still applies to anyone, even you. I want him alive. Make sure your men understand that. Dead and he's not worth a dime in reward."

Sweet stood and shook his head. "Not my choice, doing this. I'm an inside man. But I guess it's about time we had some law enforcement people. All right, I'll get the men. But I can't have any riders from the Diamond D."

"Suits me. They're already here searching for the bastard. Get things moving, Sweet!"

Renshew let the door slam as he walked out of the courthouse and to the boardwalk. His foreman, Jed, came cantering down the street, obviously watching for someone. When he saw Renshew he rode over and stepped down.

"We know for sure that it was the black woman, Frances, who went to that little house where Yancy got his head blown off. Yancy was posted to watch

Frances last night. She must have left early this morning sometime."

Renshew took a long breath. "I'll have to go talk with her. Too late to do anything now. She's a special case."

He swore softly as he walked down Main Street toward the small shop near the corner of First where Frances had her thriving business. She was the best seamstress in town, and the only who who did not work out of her home.

She had made Mrs. Renshew's clothes for years, and before that she had been housekeeper and Nanny to young Tom Renshew as he grew up without a mother two counties over.

Tom pushed open the door, heard the tinkle of the tripped bell above and caught the faint scent of lilacs from the sachets that always were in the shop.

Frances came from a curtained door that led to her living quarters in back of the shop. She smiled when she saw him.

"Good morning, Tom. I was sorry to hear about Edward."

"Thank you, Frances. I hope you're feeling well." He was tongue-tied and nervous. This tall, stately, proud black woman always did this to him. He was a little boy again. He would always be this way around her.

"How is Mrs. Renshew?"

"In mourning I'm afraid. She took the tragedy poorly."

"I should call on her. I've lost a son myself."

"No, I think she just needs to be alone for a time. But thank you for asking."

"All of my sympathics. You be sure to tell her."

"Yes, Ma'am." Damnit! he was still acting like a little boy. "Frances, did you dig a slug out of a man this morning?"

"Yes."

"Who was he, Frances?"

"I have no idea. I don't ask questions. It doesn't matter who the man in trouble might be. All human life is precious. I do what I can."

"That was the man who killed my son, Frances."

She stared at him and Tom Renshew withered. "Tom, I saw that Edward was not being a gentleman just before the shootout. Some say he had it coming. I don't judge. I would have taken bullets from anyone in the struggle. I don't judge. Neither should you."

She turned, picked up some cloth she was working on trying to get a sleeve set in correctly.

Tom shuffled his feet on the wooden floor. His hat had been gripped tightly in his left hand. He moved it to his right. There was nothing he could say. He turned and walked out of the shop.

Once outside he roared in anger and frustration. How did she have such a hold on him? Couldn't he outgrow that early help and training and love she had squandered on him?

He shook his head knowing he couldn't. She was the mother he never had. For him she could do no wrong, even when she had helped his deadly enemy.

He would ride with his men. He had to find this murdering bastard today so he could start the torture. Yes, he was going to torture this killer in every diabolical way he knew how until he screamed for death. An eye for an eye, just as it said in the Bible.

4

Virgin put down the frying pan and edged it into the hot coals. Almost at once the ground beef began cooking. She looked up at the tall sandy-haired man with a frown on her pretty face.

"You mean you've lost your memory? Somebody is trying to kill you and you can't remember why? You can't even remember your name or why you came to town?"

The man beside her nodded. "About the size of it. Anything you can tell me that might help?"

She tended the cooking meat, punched the potatoes as they boiled in the pot. "All I know is that somebody said you came into town on the noon stage and registered at the hotel. The next thing you were bracing the Diamond D gang of riders."

He nodded grimly.

"Not much help, is it?"

"Not much." He lifted his arm, moved it, lifted his elbow until it was shoulder high. "The old wing is feeling better. Tomorrow I've got to go into town and start finding out who I am."

"Tomorrow Tom Renshew will still be trying to kill you. Why not take another day to rest up?"

"I'll think about it. Right now I'm going to lay in the sun and have one of those naps you've been talking about until the food is ready."

"Good idea, that way I can get things ready quicker."

An hour later they both sat in the still warm afternoon sun. His arm was much better already.

"Let the body heal itself and it has a way we don't understand," she said. He had taken his shirt off and let the sun soak into his body. It was pleasantly warm but not hot.

"There is something else I don't understand," Virgin said looking at him with a small frown. "I realize you're not sure who you are, but you are a man, and you know I'm a dance hall girl . . ." She let it trail off.

The man smiled, a soft chuckle bubbled from him. "And you wonder why I haven't made some try to get your clothes off and make love to you. Right?"

"The thought had crossed my mind. I'm your slave, remember? Anything the master wants, he can have, anytime." She reached over and kissed his cheek, then lifted his hand and pressed it against her breasts. She held it there.

"The fact is after being forced on that boardwalk, and stripped and entered, I'm . . . I'm wondering a little bit if I can still do it, if I can still excite a man, still please him, take care of his needs."

She opened the blouse she wore and pushed his hand inside where his fingers closed around one large breast.

"I . . . I would really appreciate it if you would help me find out about myself. It's a shock to be raped, even if it was not as bad for me as some married woman who had only known one man."

George watched her. He sat up and opened the rest of the buttons on her blouse, spread the fabric aside and whistled soft and low. "What a beautiful matched pair! Just magnificent. Breasts are a woman's second most beautiful part next to her face." He massaged her orbs gently and she began to make small noises deep in her throat.

Her hand fell to his waist and crept around to his crotch. Virgin looked at him quickly. "Would you mind?"

He laughed softly. "I only have lost my memory, not my instincts for survival and how to deal with a sexy woman. Help yourself to whatever you can find."

She opened the buttons on his fly and investigated inside. When she found him rigid she gave a little yelp of pleasure.

She worked his turgid penis from his pants and bent and kissed the pulsating, purple tip.

When Virgin turned she was frowning slightly. "Absolutely no dirty talk. I never like to hear bad words, even when we're doing all sorts of things. All right?"

He smiled, then kissed both her thimble sized nipples which were rising and filling with hot blood. She sighed, then moved and dropped her blouse and pulled his boots off, then his pants. He sat there on the blanket they had spread out and cautiously she removed his cut-off long-john bottoms.

"Oh my lord!" she whispered. "Absolutely the most perfect, the most beautiful, the best part of any man. He's such a big one!" She stood and slipped out of her skirt and he saw that she wore nothing under it but a V of black crotch hair. She sat down beside him.

"If you don't want to talk sexy, what do we say?" he asked. Without giving her time to reply he went on. "Maybe we should talk about this new sculptor in Paris. His name is Francois Rodin. He's only a little over thirty years old, but already he's taking the art world by storm over there. He simply surged above and beyond the control of classical sculpting conventions."

She looked at him blankly, then frowned. " We don't know who you are, but you must have a good education, a college one at least. That might be a help for you to remember."

She grinned and pushed on top of him. "We don't want to hurt your wounded shoulder. I'll be gentle." Slowly she lowered one big hanging breast into his mouth. It flowed around his mouth and covered his nose before he could pull away. He chewed on the mound, sucking at the nipple, and then moved to the other one.

"I know I'm not supposed to enjoy it, but this time I do. I don't know how long it's been since I've made love just for the love of it."

She squirmed on top of him, her legs spread to allow his erection space, and then she moved lower, trapping him, teasing him as she slid back and forth across his penis.

"I definitely think he's ready," she said with a grin, then reached and kissed his cheek. He caught her head and brought it back to his, and gently kissed her lips, then again, harder, and then their mouths opened and they explored each other. When the long kiss ended she scowled at him.

"You're not supposed to kiss a whore."

"Don't talk dirty. I won't allow you to use that term again, ever. You're a lady I found on the board-walk, and that's all I want to know." He reached up and kissed her again before she could reply.

When the second kiss ended she groaned in need and swiftly positioned herself over him, then holding his shaft, she lowered her hot and wet scabbard until she had enveloped all of him and they were bound together.

"I'll never let you go!" she shouted.

He replied with a quick thrust of his hips and she picked up the motion and powered down on him. The dance continued and his hands found her breasts to massage and fondle as they worked their hips against each other.

Twice she climaxed, each time she wailed long and loud, her voice sounding like some ancient animal in the process of bringing new life to the planet, and welcoming the implantation with a blessing and a prayer for fertility.

Their bodies soon glistened with sweat as the sun beamed down. The tempo of the dance increased faster and faster, until the man was so charged up that he knew he had to explode soon. When his breath came in ragged gasps and she was bouncing so fast she was afraid she might slip off him, then the gates opened far upstream on the male, and the rush of procreation fluid shot down the ancient tubing toward the heartland of the female.

"Glorious!" she shouted. "I feel it! I can feel you start to get ready. I've never felt that before! You are fantastic."

The man concentrated on the unusual position. Another small matter he knew about the real man. He pumped upward and with each thrust came closer and closer.

Then the gate burst, his hips took over and automatically thrust and squeezed and shot his fluid upward into her waiting body, building with each thrust until the final one jolted her in the air and brought a wail of accomplishment and sorrow that the climax was almost over.

He tapered off then and his arms tightened around her back. Only for a moment did he feel pain in the shoulder, then it was gone and he marveled in the recuperative powers of the human form.

With his climax she peaked again and trembled and rattled as the spasms of joy drilled through her compact body, making her breasts shiver and shake above him until she fell on top of him mashing the twin orbs into his chest and trying to brush away the tears that came as the last of the climax tore through her like a dog shaking a bone.

She took a long, deep breath, then opened her eyes and leaned up on her arms so she could see him plainly.

"Glorious. I guess, maybe I can satisfy a man again. But once in a row is no record. I need to get you going again, right now, before your heat cools down."

"I don't do doubles," the man said, grinning up at her through his panting.

"*Doubles?* Now where on earth did you learn a naughty word like that?" Virgin shrilled with amusement. "You've been associating with some shady ladies somewhere."

"Evidently. Another thing I know about myself. But really, I usually need a little rest between."

"Wanta bet?" she crooned.

The next thing he knew her hips were grinding against him, her breasts swung in his face again and one of her hands snaked between their bodies and began massaging tenderly his gonads.

"Never work," he said.

"If it doesn't, I've got one more plan," she said, a

gleam in her eyes.

But just two minutes later, he felt the familiar stirrings, his mouth gulped in one of the hanging orbs of pleasure and he hardened again within her. She yelped for joy and then slowly rolled him over on his right arm until he was resting on top of her.

"Now, it's your party, George. You play any games you want to, enjoy yourself, be the dominating male. Think only of your own pleasure and use me however you want. You saved my life back there on that boardwalk, now I want to try to do a little to show you my appreciation."

She grinned. "You can even kiss me if you want to."

He bent and kissed her, and slowly began to grind his hips against her. Then he reached between them and found her tiny trigger and twanged it a dozen times until she roared into the longest, wildest climax she had experienced yet that afternoon. When she finished she was sweating and panting and there was nothing but adoration in her eyes.

He had stroked along with her some of the times during her gyrations.

"You didn't have to do that," she said softly.

"You said do anything to give me pleasure, right? That was one of them."

She caught his head with both her hands and held it as she stared at him.

"George, whoever you are, I can tell you something else about you. Whatever name you have, you are an honest, upstanding, gentle man, who is thoughtful of others, and not afraid to help, even at the peril of his own life. That much I do know."

She lifted her legs then, and put them on his shoulders and the movement and the new angle set him racing again. In only a few moments he had blasted his thinning seed deeply into her welcoming sheath and then fell on her in his mini-death that left him totally spent and gasping twice as hard for breath as he had before. They lay there for ten minutes before either moved. Her arms had come around his back and her cheek rested against his.

At last he stirred and she smiled.

"Ready for one more?"

He laughed and lifted away from her. He brought a large pan of water fresh from the spring and they bathed each other, then dried in the sun. Reluctantly they slipped back into their clothes as the sun slid behind the sandstone walls.

He cooked supper, beans out of a can, strips of bacon and more of the thick slabs of bread. For dessert there were apples. They sat at the side of the cave entrance as darkness came slowly to the small retreat.

He made a fire in the cooking ring. They spread out their blankets together and as the chill of the night overtook them, let the fire burn down and slid under the covers, snuggling together for comfort and warmth and with no thoughts of sex.

She reached up and kissed his cheek.

"We know a few more things about you, George. We know for sure that you are good with guns, but that you are not an outlaw. You would have joined the trio raping me if you had been that kind of a man. You are fair and just, so you must be on the side of the law. Maybe a U.S. Marshal, or a Territorial official of some kind."

"I hope so, but right now I'm not ruling out any possibilities."

"In the morning, I'll ride into town, see what I can find out and bring back some supplies. We might need to stay here for three or four days until

Renshew cools down. Right now he's still burning up with hatred. I know the man."

In the morning he was hurting again. His shoulder had developed some infection on the surface, and he had no idea what was happening inside.

"Is there a doctor in town?"

"We had one, until a month ago. Old Doc Rainey died of pneumonia. He was over sixty. Now all we have is Frances. I'll slip in her back door and see if she has any ointment for that shoulder. You rest."

He didn't need any encouragement. He waved as she hurried through the sunlight and into the other cave on her way to the horses. She would probably be gone most of the day.

When he woke up the next time it was when someone shook his shoulder. The six-gun came up in his hand as he sat up and he knew it was a reflexive action of long practice.

"It's Virgin," she said quickly. "I'm back from town and I'm alone. Put down the shooting iron."

She sat beside him just inside the cave entrance and unfolded a sheet of paper she took from inside her blouse. It had been against her skin and he could detect her sweet body scent clinging to it.

Then the words on the poster brought him back to reality in a rush.

"Five thousand dollars?" the man whispered. "Billy the Kid wasn't worth that much."

"Depends who wants somebody and how bad," Virgin said. "There are a hundred of these around town. The saloons are swarming with gunsharps all looking for you."

"I'm not running. I've got to find out who I am, and the only place to start is in town."

"But you can't go in looking the way you do. You'd be picked up by some bounty hunter in five minutes." She grinned. "So we make some basic changes." She rolled out a sack of goods on the blanket. Included were a straight razor, scissors, a comb, a bottle of hair dye, and shaving soap and a brush.

"You can't be serious."

"Deadly. We cut off your moustache, raise your sideburns to just over your ears, cut your hair half that short, and then dye what's left a rich black. Don't worry, the hair will grow back, and the dye will grow out in a few months. Better than winding up dead, which is what Renshew has planned for you."

She dug out a pair of shirts, two hats, and a pair of faded jeans. "This stuff should fit you. I took your measurements last night, as I remember."

The man stared at the razor, then shrugged. "Hell, you're right. Hair will grow back . . . but only if I'm still alive."

"I figured you'd see it the right way. I talked to Frances. She gave me a poultice for the shoulder. An astringent in it to draw out the poison. She says it will work, and she wished us luck. She said Renshew is killing, wild, crazy mad."

He nodded. "All right. Let's get busy. What time is it?"

"It's only a little after midday."

"We'll head for town as soon as I'm transformed into a new man. One thing. I can't be seen with you in town. That would be a dead giveaway."

She agreed.

"How far are we from town?"

"An hour's ride, maybe a little more."

"We'll come back here tonight. Renshew for sure

has all the hotels covered. I couldn't stand a chance of getting a room. If he had any question about me, he'd look for a shot-up shoulder. So we come back. How long will this take?"

An hour later they were riding for town. He looked totally different. Jet black hair showed under his hat. His eyebrows were dark, and his face was painfully clean shaven. He wore a different hat than he had before. He had lost the first one somewhere along the line.

The jacket was well worn and range-wear style, so were the jeans. He kept his boots which were Western but not with the high heels needed for real ranch work. He looked in a small hand mirror Virgin gave him, and for a moment he was startled at his appearance. He had seen his other face only in the reflection of the pool, but now he was remarkably different.

She showed him how he should slouch to help disguise his height, and his walk took on a casual pace that would not attract attention. They had treated his shoulder and put on the poultice, then a salve. The arm *did* feel better. The new shirt covered the bandage and from outward appearances he was not wounded.

The jolting walk of the horse pained his shoulder, and by the time they got to town it was aching again. They had come into the small Western town from opposite directions. He stopped at a saloon and had a whiskey to help kill the pain.

He used the one twenty dollar gold piece he owned to pay for the first and second shots of whiskey, then left and found the stage office. The driver who had been on two days ago was there getting ready to go out again. He asked the driver about the man who was in the shootout.

"Damn, you see that? Never saw a man with more moxie in my life. Stood up to those three guns just calm as daylight. Then seemed to me like a fourth gun was the one that shot him. He hadn't been off my stage more than three or four hours. Wish I got his name, but now it's probably too late."

"Why's that?"

"Why? Town's been flooded with bounty hunters, the sheriff put out a twenty man posse, and the Diamond D ranch has twenty or thirty men camped just outside of town running day and night patrols looking for him. He's either dead, caught or running like hell. If I was him I'd be arunning."

He thanked the driver and moved on to the hotel. He let his subconscious guide him. Without knowing why he walked up to the Far Northern Hotel and asked about rooms. The clerk turned the registrar around for him to sign.

"Oh, I can't register just yet, but I'm thinking about the man who was on the stage yesterday and got involved in that shootout. I heard his name was James Parker; is that right?"

As he said it, George edged a five dollar gold piece across the counter. The room clerk smothered the coin and laughed. "Not a chance. I checked him in a couple of minutes after the stage came in and then he had a meal in our dining room and had a nap after that. He couldn't have been on the street more than ten minutes when the shootout started."

"His name isn't Parker?"

"Not a chance, it's McCoy, Spur McCoy. He's some kind of lawman, I can spot them a rod and a half off."

The man's eyes slid down the list of names until he found Spur McCoy. There wasn't even a flicker of recognition. He saw the number of the room across from it, 22. There was a note that he had paid for five days in advance. All the gear should be there.

The man shrugged and looked back at the room clerk. "If he comes in, I'd like to talk to him. I'm a journalist. There should be a story in it. I'd include you, too, of course."

The clerk's interest zoomed.

"Ain't seen him around, but I'll watch for him. Hope he stays alive long enough for you to talk to him."

The man who now knew that his name was Spur McCoy faded from the hotel, stopped at the hardware store and bought a skeleton key and meandered down the block.

Five minutes later he slipped up the back stairs of the Far Northern Hotel to the second floor. A man sitting in a chair at the end of the hall eyed him for a minute, then went back to a book he was reading. Down the hall he saw a second door that was open an inch. Both men could see the door to Room 22 easily.

Spur McCoy walked casually up to the man in the chair.

"Are you Abe Johnson?" Spur asked casually.

"Hell no, get out of here, I'm busy."

When the man looked up at Spur all he could see was the muzzle of the .44 Spur held an inch from his right eye.

"I like to see a man who is good at his work. Now if you don't want your brains sprayed all over the wall, stand slowly while I remove your hog leg, and we'll go for a walk."

"Easy!" the man gurgled.

Spur took the book reader's weapon and prodded him down the hall. At the cracked open door on Room Eighteen, Spur kicked the panel open and slammed the chair sitter into the room. Spur came right behind him, his .44 covering a man who had been jolted against the wall by the force of the door blasting open. His hand was only half way to his weapon.

"Draw that piece and it's the last move you'll ever make!" Spur hissed at him.

5

The man who had been watching Room 22 from behind the partly opened door heard Spur McCoy's warning not to draw his six-gun and slowly brought both hands over his head.

"What the hell you doing, busting into my room this way?" the man demanded.

Spur turned him around, slid the hog leg out of its holster, then slammed it down across the man's head, driving him to the floor unconscious. He tied up the watcher from the hall, then tied the other man and gagged them both. He closed the door to the room gently and went on down to 22.

There were no more doors partly opened, no one else watching. Renshew must have figured two men could do the job. He was wrong.

The skeleton key opened the door lock on Room 22 and Spur pushed the panel inward so he could see in the room. No one was there. He stepped inside and closed the door, locking it and leaving his key in the slot on the inside.

Quickly he checked the room. A leather Gladstone

traveling bag filled with clothes and a Colt .45 lay open on the bed. Next to it was a Spencer repeating rifle. No clothes had been hung up or put in the dresser yet. Spur stared at the things, but could remember nothing about them. He checked the room quickly, the small closet, around the washstand, in all the dresser drawers. He found nothing else. He closed the suitcase, picked up the Spencer and moved to the door.

Cautiously he unlocked it and eased the panel open an inch. Nobody was in the hall. He couldn't be sure about watchers behind doors. He drew the .44 and held the Spencer and bag in the other hand and edged into the hall, then walked quickly to the stairs and down the steps to the side entrance and into the street.

From every tree and wall he saw a good likeness of himself staring back at him from the wanted posters. His first urge was to tear them down, but he knew that would attract attention. He knew what he came here to find out.

A pistol shot half a block away brought him up short. Spur stared in that direction and found a man with a gun out who was holding a second man against the front of a store. The words came through plainly.

"He sure as hell looks like the drawing on the wanted poster, don't he? Gonna march this sombitch over to the Golden Door Saloon and see what Mr. Renshew thinks. Come on your sombitch! You just might be worth a fortune to me."

The man shook his head. "I'm not the man. Mr. Renshew saw me yesterday. Believe me."

"Maybe," the gunman said. "You ain't, you can buy me a beer and we forget the whole thing. But, you sombitch, if you the right man, then I'm one hell of a rich cowboy!''

Spur watched them walk toward a saloon. He faded down a side street and around the block to where he had left his horse. He and Virgin had agreed to meet about a mile up the Souris River. They needed to be there by three o'clock so they could get back to the cave before dark.

Spur McCoy? He said the name out loud several times. He did not have a flicker of recognition. Spur was a Western sounding name. He wondered how he got it. McCoy was pure Irish.

When he rode out of town, no one bothered him. He slouched in the saddle and grinned a lot. When he stopped at the meeting place under a gnarled oak tree by the river, it was fifteen minutes after three.

He lay on the sparse green throwing rocks in the water and trying to remember everything he could. He had spouted off about Rodin yesterday, a sculptor in Paris. He spoke the King's English well, with good grammar and a vocabulary much larger than most of the cowboys would use.

So he could be a lawman from the East?

No, that didn't figure. He knew the West. He knew weapons. And he wasn't afraid to use one. He had killed two men, evidently, and he certainly took care of those two in the hotel. That had been pure reflex. He hadn't thought what to do, he just let his natural actions take over and put the two men down quickly.

Virgin said he must be a lawman.

Could be. Lawmen or outlaw, he must be one of the two. But outlaws could be soft and tender and sensitive, too. He stared at the Gladstone bag tied to the back of his saddle. There could be something in there that would help him. Papers, orders, letters, anything written down. He was about to stand and open the bag when he heard hoofbeats.

From long, ingrained habit he ducked behind a rig rock and peered around it at the horse. It was the same bay that Virgin rode into town, and a few moments later he was sure it was she on the mount's back. She came along and he could see no one trailing her.

He sat on the rock and reached for his shirt pocket. His brows lowered in concern. Why had he reached there? To get a cigar? To get the makings for a cigarette? He wasn't sure if he smoked or not, but the movement indicated that it was a possibility. The suitcase. It might give him some clues.

When Virgin rode up she slid off the horse and gave him a quick hug.

"I'm so relieved that you got in and out of town safely. I worried every step of the way." She pointed to the bag. "You found your belongings?"

"I did. From what the room clerk in the hotel says, my name is Spur McCoy. Does that ring a bell?"

Her head snapped up, her eyes bright. "Spur McCoy? You're kidding." She came closer, turned his face, looked at his profile, then again at his full face. Slowly, she began to chuckle, then she giggled and then she threw her arms around him and kissed his lips.

"Spur McCoy! Yeah, yeah! I spent some time in Santa Fe and in Denver. Hell, McCoy, half the people west of the Mississippi know about you. Damn near all the outlaws know you. Like I told you last night, you're some kind of a lawman, a Federal lawman, and you've got a rep that must be part brag because it's so good."

He stared down at her. "You sure?"

"Just about. Are you any good with that six-gun? Let's see how fast you can draw and put two slugs into that oak tree over there."

He shrugged and let his right hand hang loose.

"Now!" Virginia yelped.

His hand moved up to the butt of the weapon so fast she hardly saw it, the hog leg came out of leather, his thumb already half cocking the weapon that changed directions from up and back to forward in a smooth, easy draw.

His finger caressed the trigger and even before his elbow was straight, the weapon fired twice, both slugs slapping hard into the center of the oak tree thirty feet away.

Virgin ran to him and hugged him tight, then stretched up and kissed his cheek.

"Hi there, Spur McCoy! I told you that you were one of the good guys!" A tear edged down her cheek. "I just knew it!"

"McCoy? I don't even think I *look* Irish. Spur? Where the hell did I get a name like that?"

"Probably from spurring shady ladies, you naughty boy." She hugged him again, then stepped back. "Well, Spur McCoy. No wonder you raced up to defend me there on the boardwalk. Yeah, it figures. Your rep is that you're tough as a trail-ride saddle, but fair and honest. They also say you're a lady killer." She smiled softly. "I can testify to that." She rubbed her breast. "Come on, let's get back to our secure little cave."

They rode.

Spur went the rest of the way deep in thought. So he knew who he was, a lawman, a federal lawman. That could be. If so, why was he here? What was he doing in this Northern Dakota Territory village? That was his next job, find out why he had come here in the first place. Then he would settle matters with Renshew and if possible, then get on with his assignment.

"Assignment," he said softly. Yes, that had a familiar ring. Somebody sent him a telegram every so often to tell him what to do. Yes, he received an assignment from Washington, D.C. He nodded and grinned. He was starting to remember a little of it. He hoped there might be something in the suitcase that would help even more.

A half hour later in the cave, they opened his suitcase and went over the items in it. The clothes stirred faint memories but that was all. He looked over the Colt .45, hefted it, and it felt right and "at home" in his hand. He replaced the .44 in his holster with the .45 and changed the rounds in the belt to match the larger caliber.

There was a pad of paper, and the start of a handwritten letter to somebody called General Halleck in Washington, but the name meant nothing to him.

"Not much help," Virgin said as they closed up the Gladstone bag.

"At least I have some more clothes, and my shaving outfit. I might just start growing a full beard."

She stared at him a moment, then nodded. "Yes, full but kept trimmed short at a half inch or so. That would make you just devastatingly handsome!"

She laughed then and he looked at her quickly.

"I was remembering Santa Fe. Three of us girls in one of the saloons plotted how we could catch you and get you with us in your hotel room some night. We were certain that you could more than take care of all three of us at once and for all night. It was just an idle dream we had between customers."

"I thought we weren't going to talk about those

days anymore. That part of your life is over. Your father should be horse whipped. You never had a chance to do anything else. I intend to see what we can do to help you change your profession. There are a lot of women who work in the business world these days. And that way you won't risk the probabililty of getting cut up or killed."

She blinked back tears. "Nobody has ever said things like that to me before. You don't know what kind of an anchor you're putting on your rowboat, sailor."

"I know, and it's damn well about time somebody did you a good turn. Now, to practical matters. We need to stay here another day, then I think I can be in town without any problems. I'll get a hotel room and you can stay there. I don't want you to go back to the saloon you worked in."

"Yes sir," Virgin said softly, wonder in her eyes.

"Hey, pretty lady, I'm hungry. What do we have for supper around this old Indian cave?"

It broke the mood and they both laughed and began getting supper ready as the light faded in the chimney outside the cave. She took a coal oil lantern from the sack of goods she had brought back and lit it, throwing light around the cave.

She had stopped at the meat market and brought fresh cut steaks for them, more bacon and a sack of canned goods.

"At least we won't starve. What am I offered for canned slices peaches for dessert?"

He bent and kissed her cheek.

"Paid in full," she said smiling and again brushed a small tear from her cheek. Virgin was so happy she couldn't believe it. Nothing had *ever happened to her this good,* not ever!

* * *

Clete Johnson sat on the dark roan. The gelding was short-coupled with a rough gait, but she was built for stamina and one of the best cutting ponies Clete had ever owned. In his work that was a necessity. He was a professional rustler.

Clete stood only five feet three inches tall, and he packed an old Army Colt .45 that he could shoot as straight as any man alive, if he had the time. He was not a quick draw artist and knew it.

He sat on his saddle next to the small camfire well south of Minot and stared at the coals.

"A big haul, boys. We're going to make a big haul this time and get on to an easier life. I'd dern near twenty-four now, maybe a little over. Time I was moving into town and finding me some good way to make a living."

"But not an honest way, right, Clete?" Murdock jibed.

"Depends how easy it is," Clete snapped. "I ain't got nothing against honest. Like I say, it's got to be easier than this."

"What was the name of this big outfit we're gonna hit, Clete?" Murdock asked.

"Diamond D. The old man thinks he's a hot pistol. Corralled half the damn state up here. He'll never miss a thousand head, if'n we take them at the right time. When he does realize they gone, we'll be in Kansas City kicking up our heels in some fancy whorehouse."

"Damn long trail drive, Clete."

"You know where we can sell a thousand head quicker than moving them down to the railroad?" Clete asked.

Nobody spoke. Seven other men sat around the fire. They had been with Clete for six months now, and nobody had ever gone hungry.

"This is the situation. I was in town today. Old man Renshew is crazy because his oldest son got himself killed in a gunfight. He's got every man on his ranch in town hunting this killer. So we got damn near an open hand.

"Tonight we move out and check the herd we want. Tomorrow night at the latest we move in on the critters and start driving them down the line to the railroad.

"Murdock, you come with me for the scouting mission. Then we'll lay low and tomorrow night get into action."

An hour later the two riders had brushed past the outer signs on the Diamond D spread and learned that the herd of about a thousand head were still penned into a small valley that acted like a box canyon. They had strung three strands of barbed wire across the quarter mile entrance to the valley.

"No problem," Murdock said. "We cut the wire at every post and drive the critters through."

Clete and Murdock rode closer to the herd, found a small line shack that was empty except for some canned goods. They took the cans in a gunny sack and checked the herd. There wasn't a single Diamond D rider anywhere.

"Hell, let's see how close we can get to the ranch house," Murdock said. "Might be something worth stealing in there."

"Might," Clete said. "But do you know how much a thousand head of steers are worth at twenty dollars a head?"

"Clete, you know I ain't good with figures."

"If we get a thousand head here, they'll be worth twenty thousand dollars!"

"God damn! I ain't never even *heard of that much money!*"

"We'll lose some on the way. Should have more men, but we can make it with most of them. Say we drop two hundred head, we still wind up with eight hundred head. That's sixteen thousand dollars. Half for me, the other half for the rest of you."

"Jesus, sweet Holy Mother! A thousand dollars each one?"

"About the size of it."

Clete led the way back. Instead of circling wide around the ranch house they rode to within five hundred yards of it. They didn't see a ranch hand. Clete turned directly toward the house. It was dark except for one light in the upper window. As they came closer they saw a figure standing there.

They walked their mounts closer until they saw that she was either naked or wearing an extremely thin nightdress of some sort. She stretched, lifted her breasts with her hands, then one hand crept down between her legs and she slithered to the floor and out of sight.

Murdock looked at Clete.

"Jesus! Did you see that?"

"Just some woman playing fancy fingers all by herself. You can buy a dozen better than her in Kansas City."

They turned and rode away from the ranch house, off the posted Diamond D ranch lands and back to their camp well south of Minot in a dense patch of brush along the river.

The nightly coffee was ready, and the men sat around the fire telling stories. Murdock told them about the ranch woman in the window.

"Must have been a cook or a maid or something. Damn she was stark naked looking out the window. Then she saw Clete and she dropped out of sight." Everyone laughed good-naturedly. Clete didn't stand for any rank challenge to his leadership and they all knew it.

"Hell, you can buy you two like her in Kansas City," one of the other men said. "Remember once I was there and I'd just come off a trail drive and had my hundred dollars pay. Damn, I blew it in two days.

"But it was worth it. This one German gal was terrific. She had such big tits that they sagged half way to her belly. I mean they were huge. I held her upside down so I could see them twin tits making perfect peaks.

"And talk about fuck! She could drain your old pecker until it collapsed for a day and a half. Never met a gal with more bounce and jounce than that one."

Clete slid away from the fire and rolled out his blankets. The men knew what to do about closing down the fire and the camp. They'd been with him for three months, most of them.

He curled up under his blankets and before he realized it, his right hand rubbed his crotch. In a moment he was back on the range looking up at that window. Damn she had been beautiful! They were so close he had seen her breasts.

Clete let his imagination take over and in his mind he ran up to the window and called. She leaned out and waved, then ran downstairs and out into the night. He caught her and she kissed him a dozen times. She was naked and wanting him. They lay under some bushes near the well and she pulled at his pants.

Under the blanket, Clete's hand opened his fly and caught his stiffness. The woman did the same in his fantasy. She stroked him, then took him all in her mouth.

Clete's hand under the blanket pumped faster and faster. He had never been with a woman, but he had imagined it hundreds of times. She loved him. She wanted him!

His hand stroked again and again, but he kept no movement from showing on the blanket. He was just out of the firelight and this made it all the more exciting.

He could feel the woman sucking him, bouncing up and down, his prick pushing down her throat with every thrust. Then she squealed and he exploded ramming his hips forward, his hand pumping on his stiff penis.

He caught the cum in his hand as it gushed out. Clete moaned softly, his hips pumping twice more, then he held himself gently as he panted there under the thin blanket on the plains of Dakota Territory.

He sighed and gasped for more breath. Damn but she had been pretty, and *naked*! Maybe in Kansas City he'd get up nerve enough to go to a saloon and get a girl. Maybe. He was afraid the girl would laugh at him.

That he couldn't stand. He shivered, then pulled his knees higher in a fetal position and tried to sleep. But he was still excited, all worked up, still thinking about the real live woman in the window.

In Kansas City for sure. He'd get laid in a whorehouse for sure. He'd go with Murdock. With that settled, he thought about the raid. Tomorrow night would be ideal. The Diamond D would not even miss the steers for three or four days. By then they would be well down the trail and out of the Dakotas.

Clete kept fantasizing about the drive, about what he would do with all of the money they would make! Money! It was tremendously important to him.

6

That same night, Tom Renshew was not in town hunting the killer of his son, nor was he at the big ranch house on the Diamond D. He was nearly fifteen miles north along the Souris River, working up a small draw that had at the top a twisted, lightning shattered tree of uncertain species.

Twice before Renshew had been here. Tonight he led a pack horse with bundles tied on each side of the animal. Renshew rode confidently, moving closer and closer to the area that the Yanktonai Indians claimed as their private hunting grounds.

Renshew urged the pack horse up the final slope and dismounted under the gnarled, twisted hulk of a tree. He tied the pack horse beside his and stared up at the Big Dipper. It was only a little after eight o'clock in the evening and barely dark this time of the summer.

Renshew stretched and when his arms came down he saw with a start that a nearly naked Indian brave stood in front of him with a foot long knife blade's point touching his chest right over his heart.

The Indian's face held war paint, he had a single eagle's feather in a black cloth headband. His body glistened with bear grease and more paint adorned his legs and arms. He made a terrible face and screamed a war cry of the Yanktonai tribe.

Silently six more braves, all wearing war paint and waving repeating rifles, appeared around the white man and his two horses.

"Kill!" the leader shouted.

The Yanktonai braves screeched and aimed their rifles at Renshew as they danced wildly around the white chief.

Tom Renshew showed no fear. In fact he laughed and clapped the brave on the back, forgetting for a moment how the man hated to be touched. The brave jumped away, shaking his knife.

"Enough!" Renshew bellowed. His sudden roar quieted the Indians. The one with the eagle feather stepped back beside Renshew and shrugged.

"It is thrill of hunt that we here," the Indian said slowly in half remembered English.

"You come for the goods," Renshew countered. "We both know why you come, the goods and perhaps a white girl you can train to be a white squaw. No matter."

"You have?" the Indian asked.

Renshew motioned to the packs along the sides of the pack horse and two Indians sliced through the small ropes that held the packages in place. They lifted them to the ground and unwrapped them.

Even in the half light of the quarter moon, they could see the ten repeating Spencer rifles.

Dog Piss, the young warrior who had won distinction in battle when he was only fifteen, looked at the weapons. He picked up one, checked it, worked the lever and saw that there were no rounds in it. He snarled something to another warrior and looked at Tom Renshew.

"You promise many rounds."

"Two hundred rounds—in the small boxes under the last weapon."

Dog Piss checked the boxes, nodded, spoke softly to his men who bundled the rifles again in their canvas wrappings and loaded them on the pack horse.

"We take horse, too," Dog Piss said.

Renshew shrugged. One old horse more or less . . . "You understand what you are to do?"

Dog Piss stared at Renshew a moment, then nodded. "Five ranches, all in D land. Tomorrow, no more."

"Whatever you need to do," Renshew said. "Spare me the details." His face twisted a moment, then he smiled. "I have a present for you." Renshew took from his pocket a twenty dollar gold piece with a hole drilled in it. Through the hole there was a silver chain to complete the necklace. The chain was large enough to go over the Indian's head.

Dog Piss put the necklace on, showed the other braves the shiny gold coin. It would become a good luck amulet for him, depending how well the raid went tonight.

Dog Piss raised his rifle and screeched something in his own language, and the warriors suddenly disappeared, to return a moment later mounted and leading Dog Piss's horse. He leaped on the bareback mount and caught the reins that controlled a rawhide hackamore. He looked at Renshew only a moment, then he screamed a fighting litany as he led his men down the draw and back to the grasslands.

Renshew watched them only a few seconds, then

he turned and followed them. He had no conscience about what he had just set in motion. What had to be done, had to be done. It was for the security and future of the Diamond D Ranch as the biggest and most powerful spread in the Dakota Territories. He did it all for his sons. He grimaced. For his one son.

Dog Piss led his seven men down the draw, then quieted them as they took the pack horse into dense brush and tied it to a tree. They would be back this way for the prize before returning to their camp. Then they rode onto the prairie. They had ten of the white man's miles to cover before the first raid. Five of them! It would be a victorious raid, a thrill of the fight, of making coups, of using the white man's own weapons against him.

The old chiefs did not understand. They knew only of reservations, and trying to live with the Great White Father, and of starving bellies and the tribe being pushed farther and farther from its traditional hunting grounds.

An Indian tribe without the hunt, without the buffalo, without the freedom to follow the herds was no tribe at all. He, Dog Piss, would never be a lackey of the white men!

An hour later they let their ponies rest in the shadows of the trees along the river. Three long arrow shots across the river lay the first ranch. They would steal all the horses, and come back and drive away what cattle they could. He had been told not to take any of the white man's deer, but the cattle should be stolen if possible.

Lights still glowed in the small ranch house. There were only three men there, a woman and some children. Dog Piss was not worried about the men. His braves would quarrel about who got to kill them.

Ten minutes later they lay in wait around the house. Before the first raid, Dog Piss had to plead with the young bucks to come with him. They were afraid of fighting at night. Everyone knew that if a warrior was killed when Mother Sun could not smile on him, his spirit was doomed forever to remain in his body, and could not be released from a high hill to float into the great beyond.

Only when Dog Piss guaranteed that there would be no real warriors to fight them, and that they would not be even wounded, let alone killed, would the bravest of his friends come along.

One of the white men opened the back door, and the screen slammed. A man walked through the soft, warm night toward the small square house behind the cabin.

A soft twang of a bowstring sounded and the white man grabbed his chest where the arrow penetrated. A moment later a second warrior leaped on his back and slit his throat with one slash of a knife.

Man For A Woman threw a burning torch on the roof of the small house and two minutes later two more men ran outside screaming something about water.

Arrows cut them down before they reached the well. The woman came out with a child in her arms and holding a second by the hand. She ran away from the fire which now burned brightly and lighted up the whole yard.

Three Yanktonai braves closed around her, but a sharp word from Dog Piss stopped them from touching her. He moved inside their circle and stared at her. A curt gesture from him and one brave grabbed the two year old boy and tore him from his mother's grasp.

She screamed. Dog Piss slapped her hard on the

cheek. She wailed and shrunk back, touched a brave
and moved forward, away from him. The house
burned brightly behind them. Dog Piss stepped
closer to her.

"No hurt," he said in English. Dog Piss was proud
of his English words. They made him the contact for
the tribe with the round eyes.

A flicker of hope showed in Darlene Turner's eyes.
She held the baby tightly in her arms. Then before
she could move, an Indian grabbed her from behind,
his hands around her throat. Other's caught her
arms and pulled them down. Dog Piss caught her
baby girl as she struggled to hold it.

Dog Piss shook the blanket off the small child.
Held it by one leg and listened to it scream for a
moment. Then he whirled the baby around his head,
ran toward the house and threw the small girl into
the furiously burning cabin.

Darlene Turner fainted. She didn't see her two
year old son hacked to pieces with knives.

When she fainted, Dog Piss worked quickly, stripping the clothes from her. He was always amused at
the layers of clothes the white women wore. Soon all
of them were cut off. She was slim and well propor-
tioned with good breasts and long, slender legs.

Quickly he spread-eagled her, driving stakes into
the soft ground to tie her hands and feet to, then he
flipped aside his breach cloth, knelt between her legs
and mounted her.

The braves around him hooted and screamed. He
yelled at them to get the horses and check on the
cattle. Then he rubbed his face on her white breasts
and grunted and hammered his erection into her
until he was panting and grunting with satisfaction.
He climaxed a moment later and the woman below
him came back to consciousness.

Darlene Turner saw the heathen over her, felt him inside her and knew at once that she would never live through the night. She screamed. She spit at him. She yelled every vile word she had ever heard at him, but he only laughed, and slammed into her harder.

Then to her relief he pulled away from her. It was over. She was still alive. But no more had she taken a deep breath and looked around for her children, then a different brave fell on her, bit her breasts savagely, then entered her anus and she screamed and fainted from the pain.

Dog Piss moved quickly when he left the woman. He supervised the rounding up of the six horses from the corral. They were fitted with the white man's bridles, and put on a lead rope taken from the barn. More rope was found, and it was claimed and tied to the captured horses. The rest of the barn was looted of anything they could use, including two axes, a shovel, a big hammer and the long, thin iron things the white men called nails.

Then the barns were torched, the horses led away and five of the Indians rode out to the south again toward another ranch only five miles away. Two of the Yanktonais had not used the woman yet. They would catch up. The last brave to have her would slit her throat at the moment of his climax.

Dog Piss thought of the booty they had. Next time they would loot the house before they burned it. He needed cloth and dresses for his squaw. She had become taken with calico. The Yanktonai rode swiftly, trailing the captured horses.

When they returned to their camp far to the north, they would tell of grand battles and the big raid on their ancient Indian enemies, the Sioux, when they were victorious and captured many horses.

The second place the braves raided was nothing but a poor farm where the roundeyes had dug into Mother Earth, tore up the grass and tried to plant new grass. It made no sense to Dog Piss.

They listened at the walls of the square tipi for several minutes. There were only three roundeyes there: one man, a woman and a child. They silenced the dog outside with arrows, then pounded on the door. When the man foolishly opened the door, Dog Piss shot him with his rifle and they rushed inside.

They had the roundeye's lanterns which gave much light. Dog Piss ordered the braves outside with the youngster of six, then he stripped the screaming woman

She was fat, with rolls of grease under her skin, and huge overflowing breasts. The white woman bellowed and ranted and scratched him and cried, wailing all the time.

Dog Piss threw her on the white man's bed and spread her legs. She was so fat he had trouble entering her, but at last he found her slit and rammed inside.

As soon as he was in her she stopped screaming and began laughing. He didn't understand. She should be terrified. He sliced her arm with his knife. She looked at the blood and laughed all the harder.

Dog Piss was humiliated at a white squaw laughing at him. He glared at her, then cut her again and again. Quickly he came out of her, and went on slicing her thick, fat body until she was covered with running blood.

Last he sliced her throat and watched her die. He caught up her dresses from a box on the wall, found the man's rifle and set fire to the house with the lamp.

The other braves were angry with him, but he

screamed at them that the fat woman was crazy, she would weaken their spirits if they used her. It satisfied them and they took the only two horses from the barn, burned it to the ground and rushed on toward the next ranch where they hoped there would be more horses. Dog Piss told his men he thought there would be two white women at the next ranch. That was enough to satisfy them for the moment as they rode on.

It was nearly noon the next day when the first report came to Minot. A cowboy riding the grubstake line rushed into the sheriff's office with the news about a ranch family about seven miles north that had been slaughtered.

"Blood everywhere! Had to be Indians. I brought in some of the arrows. Look at those things! They're practically works of art. So round it looks like somebody put them on a wood lathe."

Sheriff Sweet took down what the cowpoke said, thanked him and told him there would be an investigation and a report sent to Washington D.C.

"It's happened before, the Yanktonai used to be peaceful, but lately some of the renegade bucks been having a field day." The sheriff paused and glanced up over his eyeglasses.

"Did you stop by at the Diamond D about five miles north of town?"

"Oh, sure did. Everything was fine there. I told them about the other place. They sent a rider over to look."

The sheriff gave the cowboy two dollars for a witness fee and told him to ride south out of town before sundown. The cowboy knew what that meant and said he'd be on his way as soon as he had a good meal.

By four that afternoon more reports came in. There had been a total of five Indian raids. All were on small ranches or sod-buster homesteads north of town. The closest was seven miles from town, the farthest about twelve. Grimly the people began counting up the toll. Seven dead at one ranch, a family of five and two hands; three at a small farm, four at another ranch, but only three bodies were found.

The total was twenty bodies. The sheriff sent out work parties to bury the dead on the ranches and erect wooden markers. There was nothing more to be done.

The preacher in town called for a service that evening for the poor souls who had been wantonly snatched from the hearts of their fellow Christians.

None of the dead had relatives in town. All had moved into the area within the past year.

Virgin had come to town to test the waters just after noon, and she heard the talk. She remembered this happening before. It was always blamed on the Indians.

She remembered the last time the mayor of the town had sent a rider to Fort Berthold down by Lake Skakawea. The commander there said he had troubles in his immediate area, and could not risk even a platoon to investigate. It was the last they heard from the army.

Dakota Territory had no militia to send. Everyone had simply held their breaths that time and waited.

Virgin almost cried thinking about the poor women. It was no secret what happened to captured white females before they were killed. She rode back to the cave with the news, but also with a good report for Spur. After she told him about the raid, she went on.

"I think we can move back into town. I didn't see the men wandering the streets looking at every stranger the way they were before. The hysteria has worn off. Now the people have something new to talk about."

Spur paced around the fire. "I thought the Yanktonai were settled down on some territory around the Canadian border. What got them riled up?"

"Renegades probably," Virgin said. "It's something we just learn to live with being this close."

Spur snapped a piece of branch in half and dropped it on the small fire. "Well, I can't take on the whole territory, anyway. Let's get moved back to town so I can dig into the real reason I'm here. There must be somebody in town who knows."

It took them two hours to get things packed up, the cave cleaned up and the horses walked back to town. They came in separate ways and agreed to meet in front of the Far Northern Hotel about dusk.

Spur tied up his horse at the rail in front of the hotel as soon as he arrived, registered as George Harding and got not a second glance from the same room clerk he had bribed the day before to look at the register.

He saw his room number was 29 and he went up. There were no men watching Room 22 today; in fact he saw no one watching on any of the floors. Either Renshew had given up in his search or he was using better tactics.

Just before dusk Spur went downstairs, found Virgin in a conservative dress and a hat that covered most of her face.

"Remember, I'm a sporting woman in this town. You can't be seen taking me to your room."

They went up the back stairs, Spur ordered two dinners brought to his room and they dined in style. Just as they finished, someone knocked on the door. Spur went to see who it was.

A man about thirty-five stood there, hat in hand. He was nearly bald and had the soft white skin of an indoor man. He looked up and smiled.

"Excuse me for barging in, but I can't wait any longer. My name is Ray Krause. I run the hardware and ranch supplies store in town. I know you're really Spur McCoy and I think I know why you came to Minot."

7

Spur McCoy grabbed Krause by the coat front and pulled him inside the room, then he closed the door. At once Spur let go of Krause and straightened his jacket.

"Sorry," Spur said grinning. "You said you know why I'm in town, that's a highly important subject to me. I'd offer you a drink if I had one. What exactly do you know about why I'm here?"

Krause's look of sudden fear eased and he smiled for a moment. "I'm not certain, but I am glad to know that you are the same Spur McCoy who came in on the stage two days ago. Your disguise is good, it has everybody fooled."

"Thanks, but what's my job here in Minot?"

"Why, the Indian raids, of course. I figured you knew."

"The Indian raids? Like the five attacks on the settlers last night?"

"Right," Krause said. "I wrote to the Governor and to the Speaker of the House of Representatives and to our Territorial observer in the U.S. Senate and to the Vice President. It's a dirty situation here and we need to have it straightened out. Now we just lost twenty more people."

"But, Mr. Krause, if it's Indians, that's the army's job, isn't it?"

"Not this time. The way I figure it somebody is urging the Indians on, maybe even supplying them with rifles to help do the job."

"Gun running to the Indians? You have any proof?"

"Nothing but circumstantial, that's the problem. I know for damn certain who is doing it, but I can't prove it. I'm not about to stick my neck out just to get it blown off."

"Who would benefit by the Indian raids?" Spur asked. "Surely not the town."

"You work on it, you'll come up with some idea. Now I got to get back home. My Ida doesn't like me to be gone long after dark." He smiled at Virgin knowing who she was but not saying anything. Then he slipped out the door.

Spur stood there for several seconds scowling, then he went to his Gladstone bag on the bed, opened it and dumped everything on the patchwork quilt.

"There must be something here identifying me. If I have orders to come here, where are they?"

They went through his clothes, found a small notebook but it held only blank pages.

And the end of fifteen minutes they sat on the bed amid his unfolded clothes and shaving gear. They had found no documents.

"There must be something." He looked at the Gladstone again. It was the highest quality luggage available. Why was he using it? He went over the inside carefully testing seams on both the sides, prying, lifting.

Everything was solid.

He moved to the bottom of the case. The second stitched seam he tested was loose. He pulled at it and found it moved. One more tug lifted a section a foot square in the bottom of the bag. Under a thin metal plate, covered by the leather facing, he found an inch-deep secret compartment. In there were several papers, letters and a stack of hundred dollar bills.

"You've found it!" Virgin squealed.

He took out the papers and looked through them. He indeed was Spur McCoy, a special agent for the United States Secret Service. President Abraham Lincoln had signed his commission. There were addresses in Washington where the main office was situated, and the names of his boss, General Wilton D. Halleck, and the director of the agency, William Wood.

In St. Louis he had a field office where Fleurette Leon was his assistant. Capitol Investigations was the cover name they used for their detective work.

Virgin had picked up the stack of hundred dollar bills. She counted them her eyes growing wider all the time.

"Spur! There is more than five thousand dollars here . . . in cash! I've never seen that much money."

Spur took one of the bills from the stack and looked at it. He frowned. "I did that with the thought of checking to see if the bill is genuine, as if I should know. That's one of the things I haven't remembered."

He smiled. "I am getting some fringes and bits and pieces of memory back. The bills certainly look good enough to me. I'll try one at the bank tomorrow and get some change for it. We could use some ready money."

He had been leafing through papers, now he read one and handed it to Virgin. It was a telegram sent to him in care of the station master at Cheyenne, Wyoming. She read it out loud.

"McCOY. GO TO MINOT, DAKOTA TERRI-TORY. INVESTIGATE GUN RUNNING TO YANKTONAI INDIANS. NO SUSPECTS. CON-TACT SOONEST. HALLECK."

Spur rubbed his chin with his hand. "Now I know for sure what my job is, all I have to do is find out who is smuggling the weapons to the Yanktonai and stop them. Simple. In the meantime I hope I get some of my memory back so I know how to go about doing the job."

Virgin moved closer to him so her thigh touched his. "Hey, could I say something?"

He grinned his approval.

"I've watched a lot of men rather closely the past few years. I've been watching you. You might have lost some of your memory, but the instinctive, learned, know-how of what to do and how to do it is still there. Like shooting, like trailing, move-ment, caution. You can do anything you decide to do."

Spur reached down and kissed her.

"Is that a promise?" she asked.

"That's a guarantee. Just as soon as I get this mess cleaned up and check out a couple of saloons. As I remember, a man can learn a lot by having a quiet beer in a saloon and listening to the talk at the bar."

He learned almost nothing at the Queen of Spades Saloon. The beer was warm, two girls shilled drinks and vanished upstairs from time to time. One half-drunken cowboy braced a towner thinking he looked like the picture of Spur on the wanted poster. He was hooted down and the barkeep threw him out on the street.

The frenzy about making five thousand dollars had died down. But Spur knew the serious bounty hunters were simply laying back, watching and waiting. The danger was still there, and more potent now than it had been before. Nobody questioned him.

There were outbursts of hatred against the Yanktonai. The redmen were generally considered a bunch of worthless heathens who should be wiped out.

"Yeah, you want to go up to Grand Tree and blast them out of that mountain fortress they have?" one voice called. "The damn army would play hell getting half way to their lodges."

When he went back to his hotel room, Spur realized that he had not heard one word about how the Indians got the rifles, or any hint about anyone in town supplying them. Was it a taboo subject, or hadn't anyone but Ray Krause thought about it?

Back at his hotel room, he found Virgin sitting naked on the bed playing solitaire.

He undressed and slid into bed and she moved toward him. "You didn't think you were going to go right to sleep, did you?"

"You're holding me to my promise? You're a hard woman, Virgin."

She reached between his legs and chortled. "Not nearly as hard as you are, my sweet prince."

They finally got to sleep a little after one in the morning.

Spur was wide awake and anxious to be moving by six A.M. He left a short note for the sleeping Virgin, had his morning coffee and a large, gooey, sticky cinnamon roll, then wandered the streets.

The town wasn't really awake yet. The stage was getting ready to move on. A few card games were just breaking up in two saloons. A swamper sloshed off the boardwalk in front of the biggest general store in town.

Spur wore the cowboy clothes disguise that had proved effective. He didn't even look the way he must have usually dressed. He was about to cross a street when a man rode up. He was dusty and trail worn, but still had a dignity and presence that brought immediate attention.

"Hey, pilgrim," the tall stranger called. "This really Minot, Dakota Territory?"

"Sure as hell is."

"Thought it would be bigger."

"Ain't San Francisco, that's for damn sure," Spur said.

The man was dressed for the trail, only for him that evidently meant a three piece black suit complete with vest and heavy gold chain, a British bowler, white tie and stick pin. He stepped down smartly.

"Does this hotel have beds?"

"Yep," Spur said following his country bumpkin routine. But all the time he was searching his memory for the face. He knew this man from somewhere. Colorado. He was moving in on it. The big man in the black suit, who appeared to be just a bit on the heavy side, took off his bowler to reveal a head of dark brown hair that had been recently clipped short and combed with a part on the left. Heavy brows matched the color of his thick lip hair.

"Obliged," the man said and untied a crushed carpetbag that had been laced to the saddle.

Spur had the name. He grinned. "You in town looking for somebody in particular, Mr. Masterson?"

The lawman's hand darted to his holster, but when he saw Spur's thumbs hooked in his shirt pockets; he relaxed.

"True. I don't ride this far just for exercise."

"You still at Trinidad over in Colorado?"

Again the man stiffened, then relaxed. He looked squarely at Spur. "Yes, I'm at Trinidad. Do I know you from somewhere?"

"Not so you would remember, Sheriff. Lots of folks know a famous man like Bat Masterson who he don't know. You got nothing to worry about from me. I've always respected you as a lawman."

Bat Masterson did seem to relax a little. He took down the bag and checked the tie on his horse.

"If you had a mind to walk this critter down to the livery for a rub down and some oats, I'd be more than pleased to set you up to breakfast."

"Thanks, already had mine. Could go for another cup of coffee, though." Spur grabbed the reins, unwrapped them and without another word walked the tired horses toward the livery. He hadn't seen Bat Masterson for five years. He had been at Tombstone at the time during a short and wild period of that crazy and wide-open town.

Bat Masterson had been an enigma to law officers in the West ever since he first pinned on a badge. Was he a good guy or simply a bad guy hiding behind the law?

Bat got his start as a buffalo hunter, and one day out on the Kansas plains he was approached by five Cheyenne braves from Bear Shield's tribe. Most buff hunters tried to get along with the Indians. Bat saw them smiling and decided to play it slow. They came up to him and then their smiles vanished, they pushed a lance against his throat and stripped him of his pistol and his Sharps rifle, then slammed it into his forehead and left him bleeding and furious.

He rode back to his band of hunters and urged them to attack the Cheyenne to get his rifle and pistol back.

The buff hunters refused and, sensing an Indian attack, they rode off for Dodge, sixty miles north. Bat trailed then a while, the blood still stinging his eyes from the gash on his forehead. Then he turned and rode off in the direction of the Cheyenne. He found Bear Shield's camp, and waited for darkness.

The Indians owed him something and he always collected on his debts. After dark he sneaked into the rope corral, stampeded the entire camp's herd of ponies and captured forty head which he drove into Dodge.

The Cheyenne had so much trouble catching their war ponies that they couldn't organize a party to go after him.

Bat drove the ponies into Dodge and sold them for twelve hundred dollars, three years pay as a cowhand. He figured the money more than made up for losing his pistol, his Sharps and the clout on the forehead.

Spur came back from the livery, found Bat in the dining room of the Far Northern Hotel and had a cup of coffee.

"Farthest I've ever been chasing one man," Bat said softly, preening his heavy brown moustache. "Don't reckon that I'll come this far again. Especially since it looks like I'll go home empty handed. What's this about a five thousand dollar reward?"

"Just some local situation. A rich rancher's son

got killed in a shootout. Old man is screaming for blood."

"Know the type." Masterson fingered the heavy gold chain that anchored in one vest pocket and probably had a gold watch in the other. "You a lawman?"

Spur took a sip of coffee. "Now and then," Spur said.

"I don't see a badge, you must not be a local."

"That's right," Spur said. He finished the coffee. "Your breakfast should be along soon, Mr. Masterson. Good luck on your hunt."

"Going to take more than luck on this one. Never did get your name."

Spur hesitated just a second and Masterson's amused glance touched Spur. "George Harding," Spur said holding out his hand.

"Good enough. Harding, or whoever, I hope you find your man, too."

The handshake was firm, solid, friendly, and the two parted knowing they would meet again sometime.

Spur got to the boardwalk and had moved down in front of Pellison's Bakery when a man stepped out from the door and held up his hand.

"Hold it right there!" the man demanded. "You look powerful like them posters I've been seeing."

The man's eyes burned into Spur's. Moving with practiced grace, Spur pulled the Colt .45 from leather, cocked the hammer and pressed the muzzle against the stranger's chest.

"You were saying something?" Spur asked softly yet with a deadly tone that left the accuser wide eyed, his face suddenly turning white.

"Damn . . . you hardly moved . . . I didn't even see . . ." His hands lifted slowly from his sides so there could be no mistake. "Hey, second thought, you don't look nowhere like this guy. My mistake."

Spur didn't move the weapon, said nothing else. He just waited and let the pressure build.

Sweat beaded on the accuser's face. His eyes looked around in near panic now. "You're not going to kill me, are you? I only said you kind of looked . . . please, mister. I didn't mean no harm. I don't guess you look nothing like that poster. No sir! nothing like the poster picture at all!"

"You swear to that?"

"Oh, damn right! Yes sir. You don't look nothing like the poster. Swear on my mother's grave, God rest her soul."

Spur eased the muzzle away from the man's shirt.

"Turn around and touch your toes with your fingers," Spur ordered.

The man scowled, his eyes still naked with fear. He bent and touched his toes. Spur's boot slammed into his buttocks, sprawling him off the boardwalk into the dust and directly on top of fresh horse droppings in the street.

The little drama had attracted twenty onlookers. Laughter raced through the crowd. The man in the dust looked up at Spur just glad to be alive.

"Nest time you be damn sure before you accuse a man of being a killer!" Spur said sternly with a deadly ring that made two women cower back on the boardwalk.

Spur turned, touched his hat in salute to the two frightened ladies and walked on down the street toward the courthouse. He knew that he should go to the sheriff. This was his jurisdiction.

But Virgin had told him that the sheriff was a pawn of Renshew. The man would not be willing to cooperate in any way. He walked past the courthouse without even looking in. Beyond he saw the Hardware and Ranch Supply.

Ray Krause. Another talk with him might help. Two men were buying fencing and dynamite when Spur walked in. They evidently were ranchers who Krause knew. Spur waited until they had left, then he motioned to the back and they stepped behind a door that led to the stock room.

"Mr. Krause, you were right. I found my orders. My job is to find out who is running the guns to the Indians. I'm going to need more help from you. I won't let anyone know that you're helping me. That could be dangerous for you."

"I got you here, that's enough. If they ever found out . . ."

"If who found out? Who are you afraid of?"

Krause shook his head. "I've got a wife, and two kids . . ."

"I'll protect you."

"Twenty-four hours a day for five years? It can't be done. I'd be worm food within a week." Krause put down a keg of eight-penny box nails he had moved to the aisle. "Figure it out for yourself. Who benefits when the small ranchers and the home-steaders get slaughtered by the Indians?"

"I just don't know the area well enough, Mr. Krause. All I need is a name."

"I can't do that. Ask yourself where the victims lived. Who also claims to have grazing rights to those areas, those farms, those small ranches?"

"The Diamond D."

"Brilliant! Why didn't I think of that?" Krause looked up. "I didn't tell you, right? You simply used logic and figured it out."

Spur snorted and walked in a small circle. "Logical, but it's too damn obvious. Why would

Renshew set up such a plan when everyone could guess he engineered it?"

"Because he's so strong, so powerful, that he doesn't think anyone will challenge him. He's got the county in his pocket. He is buddies with the Governor. The Attorney General is married to one of his cousins. He could buy the whole damn state if he wanted to."

Spur sat on a box of bolts. He nodded slowly. "Yes, all right, I'm coming around. Obviously nothing bothers somebody with all the power he has. I agree. So it must be Renshew. Now all I have to do is prove it."

"Then let us hang him. That's all I ask. Don't kill the bastard. He owes this town, this county more than that. There have been thirty-seven people killed on these Indians raids over the past two years. Ray Renshew doesn't have enough blood to pay back all those lives, but every drop he has will be a start."

Spur held out his hand. "I'll nail him any way I can, but I promise to try my best to keep him alive for trial. I'd say the people of this county deserve that much."

8

When Spur came out of the store after talking to Ray Krause, he saw people running down the street. A shot sounded somewhere ahead of them and more people began moving that way.

Spur touched a man's sleeve as he started past.

"Sir, what's happening down there?"

"Don't know for sure. Somebody said Renshew caught the guy who gunned down his kid!"

The man brushed past Spur and hurried down the boardwalk.

Spur moved that way, a concern growing. If Renshew caught somebody he figured had killed his son, he wouldn't be particular about a trial.

A lynching!

Spur hurried then, ran with a pair of cowboys, holding his six-gun from flapping on his hip.

A block down Spur saw the center of excitement. More than two hundred people had gathered around a wagon in the middle of main street. He worked closer and soon saw that a man people said was Tom Renshew stood on the wagon's bed six feet away

from a man with a slash on his forehead, one eye
battered shut and both hands tied behind him.

The man had sandy hair, long side burns and a
moustache. He was well over six feet tall and had an
empty holster tied low on his thigh. With a little
imagination the man fit the look on the poster
drawing.

Spur had to stop this. He edged forward just as
Renshew began to shout to the crowd.

"Told you we'd find the killer who bushwhacked
my son. We got him, right here. Right size, hair is
right, gunman, and he can't account for his whereabouts when Ed was murdered.

"Our Circuit Court Judge isn't in town, so we're
having a trial by the people, right here. Just like
they used to do in the mining camps. All legal as
hell, called a governing committee.

"I've had some legal training, so I'll be the judge.
I need twelve men to volunteer for the jury. You
twelve right there, you move up here to the wagon
and listen good.

"The County District Attorney is out of town. He
should be the prosecutor. Hell, we'll do without one.
The bench will ask the questions.

"The accused calls himself Jessie. Jessie, do you
have a lawyer to represent you in this proceeding?"

Spur saw the beaten man try to talk. His voice
came as a wheeze. Spur saw the large bruise coloring
on his neck and throat. He had been hit in the throat
so hard his voice box must have been damaged.
Jessie couldn't make a sound.

"Well, guess the accused has no attorney,"
Renshew said.

"This is all illegal!" a voice shrilled from the
crowd.

"Who said that?" Renshew yelled his face red.

"The accused must have a defense counsel," the same voice screeched.

The crowd was silent.

Renshew nearly exploded but he got control of himself. "All right. Irving, you get up here. You're the killer's lawyer. Be fair and honest."

A man climbed on the wagon, and tried to talk to Jessie. The man was crying. It was plain that he couldn't speak.

Spur watched the start of the trial, not believing it. Renshew was going to lynch an innocent man! Spur knew he could never let it go that far.

Two witnesses were called. Both swore they saw the man draw and fire and kill Ed Renshew. Nothing was said of the circumstances.

"Ed was raping a woman on the boardwalk!" The shrill voice of the woman cut through a pause in the proceedings.

"Find that woman!" Renshew thundered. "She's in contempt of this court!" Some of his men worked through the crowd, but no one would point out the woman.

A minute later it was over.

"Since the accused has not denied that he killed the victim, and since the prosecution has presented two honest and true witnesses that prove the accused did in fact kill the victim, this court finds the accused guilty."

There was a hush over the three hundred people listening.

"Therefore this court passes sentence. The accused will hang by the neck until dead. The sentence to be carried out at once from the big oak tree at Second and Main Streets. Do it."

Before his words faded, Spur bellowed. "That man can't be guilty of killing Ed Renshew in a fair fight, because I killed him. I shot Renshew when he was raping a woman on Main Street in broad daylight! I demand to be heard!''

Before Spur could say more, he saw a movement beside him, then something hit him in the head and he went down. The crowd surged around him as they moved the prisoner up the street to the big oak.

A few people stepped on Spur, then someone swore like a rawhider and the people parted around him. A moment later a woman knelt beside him and put a wet handkerchief on his forehead. She rubbed his hands, patted his cheeks, then wrung the handkerchief out over his head and he sputtered and came back to the land of the living.

"What the hell?" he asked groggy, woozy. Then he remembered. "That man, the one they tried. He's innocent!"

The girl beside him nodded. He tried to focus his eyes on her. When she came sharp and true he grinned. "Virgin. I remember you. We've got to get up to that oak tree!" He reached for his six-gun. It was gone.

"Damn!" Spur shouted. "The same guy who pistol whipped me must have taken it to stop me from making trouble. Come on!"

Spur jumped up from the ground, took three steps and had to stop as the sudden movement drained blood away from his bruised head and he almost fell. He bent low for a minute to get blood back to his brain.

She held his arm as they walked toward the oak tree. The people were jeering and laughing and calling. They probably hadn't had a hanging in months.

As Spur neared the crowd he saw the man standing on the back of the wagon. Then suddenly he wasn't there.

The crowd hushed in an instant.

"No!" Spur shouted, but he knew he was too late. The farm wagon had been driven out from under the man and Jessie dangled at the end of a half inch rope. Spur saw him now, his head was at an unnatural angle.

His neck was broken. The man who tied the hangman's knot had known his business. No slow strangulation. No chance to save an innocent man.

They leaned against a store front.

"You tried," she said.

The crowd quieted as a tall man in a black suit and vest hurried up to the death wagon. He had a double-barreled shotgun over his arm.

Spur was just close enough to hear the conversation.

"Where the hell is your sheriff?" Bat Masterson barked.

Tom Renshew bristled at the man's tone. "The sheriff is out of town on business. Who the hell are you?"

"My name is Bat Masterson, I'm a lawman from Colorado. I don't have any more authority here than this double scattergun commands. But right now I don't like what I got here too late to stop. This is a damn lynching, and if I had the power, you, whatever your name is, would go to prison for twenty years!"

"Now just a minute . . ." Renshew began.

Bat swung the shotgun up, the twin, ugly black holes aimed directly at Renshew's chest.

"Give me a good reason to kill you! Right now it wouldn't take more than about two words out of your mouth." He turned away. "Cut that man down. See if he has any identification. Does anyone here know this man?''

Bat stood over a cowboy as he went through the dead man's pockets. Two sets of papers were passed to him. He read them and looked at the crowd.

"Anyone see this man in town today?"

A man shuffled forward.

"I think I know him. He looks like a gent who came in on the stage this noon." He looked closer. "Yep, that's him. Seems he said his name was Jess Urick. I was driving the stage. He was a nice kind of guy. Real quiet."

"When did the shootout take place that killed the young man Jessie was hung for?"

"Two days ago," somebody called.

"Two days ago, is that right?" The crowd roared a "yes."

"Then you've just hung the wrong man. This gentleman's name is The Rev. Jessie Urick. He was going through here heading for Devil's Lake where he was to take over the Baptist church there as its pastor."

A stir went through the crowd. Bat Masterson looked hard at Tom Renshew, who stood nearby surrounded by six men with rifles in their hands.

Masterson walked over to Renshew and thrust the papers at the flustered rancher.

"You better notify the church their pastor won't be coming. Tell them that you lynched him for a crime committed two days before he came to town. If I had the power I'd have you drawn and quartered right here in the street. I'd have horses pull you apart, tear off your arms and then your legs! You're the poorest excuse for a man I've ever seen!"

Renshew stared at him. "All right, I made a mistake."

"No!" Masterson bellowed. "You didn't *just*

make a mistake. You murdered a man, just as much as if you'd put a gun to his head and pulled the trigger. Where the hell is your sheriff? I'm swearing out a citizen's complaint against you right now!"

Spur looked at Virgin and grinned. "I couldn't have done that better myself. And you can bet that not even Renshew is going to mess around with Bat Masterson. My guess is that Renshew is going to take a long ride back to his ranch and cool his heels for a couple of days."

"I agree. Hey, have you had dinner yet? It's almost noon and I'm getting hungry. There's a little cafe down the street, a couple of blocks where I eat sometimes. Interested?"

"Yes. I'm trying to figure out my next move." She led him as they went through the clearing street away from the middle of town.

"There's an axiom that power corrupts those who have it, and absolute power corrupts absolutely. That may be about the position Tom Renshew is in. He has more power than he knows how to handle. Bat Masterson must have set him back a notch or two, but he's not really hurt. I think he's the man who's hiring the Indians to slaughter the settlers. It keeps the squatters off land he doesn't own but controls, and it puts the blame on the Indians."

They had their noon meal at a small little eating place with only two tables in the front of the house. A young Greek man and woman ran the place. Spur couldn't pronounce any of the names on the hand-written menu, but the sandwiches they ate were delicious.

"Nice change from meat and potatoes," Virgin said.

Spur looked at her remembering something. "Was that you yelling at Renshew during the mock trial?"

Virgin grinned. "Would you be mad if I said it was?"

"Not in the least."

"Good, it was me and I meant it. Say, did you mean that about trying to help me change jobs?"

"Of course."

"Good, because I haven't been to work for three nights now and I got fired."

"I'll work on that." Spur pushed back from the small table and they went to the door. "First I want to check the hotel and see about some different clothes that aren't blood splattered. Then I'll get a small bandage on the back of my head, and be ready for action."

"I . . . I want to see about a new dress. Something a little more conservative than most of mine. Frances promised me a remake on a dress somebody ordered and never picked up. I'll see you at the room before supper."

Virgin smiled as she hurried down the street to the small shop where Frances ran her seamstress business. Virgin stepped in and talked quietly with the tall, imposing black woman. Then she reached out and hugged the taller woman.

"You won't be sorry, Frances. I learn fast and I always have been good cutting out patterns. I'm sure that in a week or so I'll be more than able to pay my way. I'm determined to stay here in town and make good. I don't care what they say about me. I can stay in the back room out of sight if you want me to."

Francis held up her hand.

"Girl, don't talk to me about getting put down by folks. I been bad mouthed and pushed off sidewalks and told to move and not to go in this store and that store for all my life. Only last year or two I get any respect at all.

"You more than welcome. I'll pay you enough, and you can stay with me in the place out back, it's big enough for two. Now, first thing I want you to do is get me organized. I don't know where to find anything. Get all the cloth of one kind together and mark it and put it just so. Then we find what we want fast."

Frances watched the small girl working the rest of the afternoon. She would be good, Virgin would help a lot.

For just a moment Frances allowed herself the luxury of remembering when Tom Renshew came to the store. Tom had been embarrassed, he had been distraught, but still he had shown that he remembered her early training. It had been a strange time.

In those days most blacks were slaves. She had run away, worked her way north into the wild area that became Dakota Territory. She could cook, sew, mind a child. Will Renshew had lost his wife in childbirth. Frances became substitute mother for little Tom, mistress for his father, woman of all abilities.

When little Tom became sixteen, his father brought him to Frances's room one evening and told her to introduce the boy to the wonderful world of women. She could have refused, but she obeyed. From then on she had serviced both the Renshews until the elder died a year later.

Two years after that she bore Tom's son, who had died when he was less than two years old. It had been Tom's fault, and to this day she could make Tom Renshew tremble with a frown. When he married he brought Frances up north to Minot to live in town and set her up in a seamstress business.

Those first few years it didn't matter if she made money or not. But quickly she was a business success. She had watched Tom become more and more powerful.

Now it was too late for him. He didn't realize it, but she did. How ironic that she had dug out the bullet and saved the life of the man who killed Tom's son, and who would ultimately be Tom Renshew's downfall. She knew. She had the gift.

Virgin would so well in the business. In time the men would forget her, the town would forgive her, and she would marry and settle down or move and marry.

Frances smiled. It was strange how things worked out sometimes, most strange.

When he left Virgin on the sidewalk, Spur headed for the hotel. He stopped at the desk and found a message. It was in an envelope. He carried it up to the room and there washed off his scalp, and found only a small cut. He put some astringent on it from his shaving kit and washed his torso and hands and face.

He put on one of his casual shirts and some slacks, and felt more like his old self. More fringes of memory were returning. He remembered Fleurette Leon in St. Louis. He could picture his boss and William Wood, the agency director.

In time everything would be back. When he was presentable again, he opened the letter and looked at the delicate woman's writing.

"Mr. George Harding. I'm not sure that is your real name, but I do know why you are in town, and I can help you prove who is giving the Indians the guns. But you must do it my way. I'm a respectable married woman and I can't risk my reputation by meeting you in public.

"Please meet me at the Souris River Falls about a

half mile downstream from town. Come alone and tell no one where you are going or who you might be meeting. I am not trying to hurt you, I only want to help.

"Please come alone. I will tell you everything I can about the Indians and the guns. I hope it will be a help to you." It was signed only, "A Friend."

Spur McCoy was remembering more and more all the time. To him this smelled like a trap. Any killer could get a woman to write such a note and when Spur arrived two shotguns would hit him with double-ought buck-shot and the game would be over.

But he had to go. It could be helpful. He knew exactly how to make sure he didn't get hurt if it were a trap.

9

Spur looked at the note again. There was a P.S. that asked him to come promptly at two P.M. He checked his pocket Waterbury, it was only a little after one o'clock. His mind clicked off the possibilities. He found the old .44 Virgin had given him and slid it into his holster.

The only way to beat a trap, if this were one, would be an early arrival. He put on his hat, walked out his door and was on a rented horse from the livery five minutes later. He went out of town heading west, then circled to the south and found the falls with no trouble. The water cascaded down a six foot drop and he wondered why no one had built a small mill there to take advantage of the natural water power.

He hid his horse a hundred yards downstream and found a convenient hiding spot where he could watch the trail south along the river and the small grassy area around the falls. It looked as if it were used for picnics and outings. The small pool near the falls would probably be good for swimming.

He had arrived at twenty-five minutes after one, and now waited in his concealed position. If it were a trap the bushwhackers would arrive early as well.

Two o'clock came and went and nothing happened. A lone rider came along the road, glanced at the falls and kept moving north toward town. He probably had had a long dusty ride from the last saloon and was eager for a drink.

Fifteen minutes after the hour, Spur heard a rig coming before he saw it. It was a small buggy, pulled by one horse. The winter storm curtains were up along the sides and in front and he couldn't be sure who was inside.

The rig drove in and stopped at the falls. A moment later the curtains came down and he saw there was only one person in the rig, a woman with long blonde hair. She looked around, called softly, then got down from the buggy and walked to the water and back to the horse.

As she stroked the black mare's head, Spur stepped up beside her. She flinched as if she had been struck, then smiled.

"Mr. Harding, I would presume?" she said; her voice had a New York ring to it. She was about thirty, Spur guessed, tall, slender, with a small round face and darting eyes. She smiled and she became beautiful.

"Yes, Ma'am. That name will do for now. You mentioned something about guns and Indians?"

"Yes, I can tell you plenty, but first please drive my rig downstream a ways, past those trees so it can't be seen from the road. A lot of people know my buggy, and I can't be found talking to you."

Spur helped her into the rig. Her hand was warm and it gripped his more than needed. He drove the rig to the spot she directed and it was completely hidden from the road in either direction. They were a quarter of a mile from the south trail at that point.

She held out her hand. "My name is Pamela Sweet, I'm the sheriff's wife, but don't let that bother you. I disagree with almost everything he does, especially the lackey he plays to the great Tom Renshew."

She smiled. "Does that surprise you? Yes, there are a few of us in town who oppose Mr. Renshew." She reached in the back of the buggy and took out a picnic basket. "I brought along a light snack for a picnic, I hope you don't mind. It can be an early supper if you've had dinner."

She stepped down and he took the basket and a blanket she pointed to, and they walked south along the river until she found a spot under a big tree and where they could see the water. The South Trail was not in sight.

He spread the blanket and she sat down gracefully, the wide skirt of her dress billowing around her offering only a brief glance at a bare ankle.

She patted the spot directly beside her on the flounce of her skirt and he sat down moving the dress aside. She smiled again.

"George, there's no reason to be afraid of me. I came here to help you. But, frankly, it's going to be a trade. I have some information that you want, but you also have something that I need, so it will be mutually beneficial."

"I've been known to do some trading. You're from New York, aren't you? The city?"

Her face billowed with a smile. "Yes, you must be from that area, too! Oh, I miss the city so much. There are so few people here, and so few with any . . . any culture."

She watched him a moment, then moved toward

him until her thigh touched his.

"George, I'm not too good with words sometimes." She leaned in and kissed him hard on the mouth, her tongue caressing his lips asking to be invited inside. One of her hands rubbed his chest and she gave a long low sigh and put her arms around him.

When she ended the kiss she put her chin on his shoulder and pushed her breasts against his chest.

"George, I need you!" She leaned back and watched him. "Does that shock you?"

"No, you're a beautiful woman."

"And you're an absolutely gorgeous man! I want to see you naked! I want to hold you and be smothered by you and kiss you and have you deep, deep inside me. Do you understand?" She unbuttoned the fancy blouse she wore over the long skirt. When the buttons were open she pushed back the fabric and he saw she wore nothing under it.

Her breasts were sculptured in pure white marble. Tipped with pink nipples and soft brown areolas. They surged toward him and Spur bent and kissed each one.

"Oh, Lord, I've died and gone to heaven! My titties haven't been kissed in more than a year. Glorious, don't ever stop!"

He put his head in her lap, turned on his back and she draped over him, dangling her breasts to his mouth. Slowly he sucked one in and she moaned softly.

"Oh, *damn* but that is fine! We're going to have a beautiful afternoon!"

He sucked and chewed on both her orbs, then came up and slipped the blouse off her arms. In response he took off his vest and shirt and she squealed and massaged his bare chest and his black hair there.

"I love a man with hair on his chest, it's so sexy."

He reached down and unlaced her low shoes and slid them off, then massaged her foot. She looked at him curiously.

"Hey, that feels good, sort of warm and sexy and . . . Oh, Lord but I need you inside of me!"

He worked his hand up her leg, over the high stockings. She spread her legs as he worked higher to the softness of her inner thigh. Under the skirt she trembled and then shivered.

Her hands worked quickly and she pulled the skirt over her head. She wore no petticoats, no drawers. Her tall, lush body was naked, her legs milk white, without a blemish. Her calves were rounded but slender, her thighs sturdy and well formed. A large black triangle of black fur covered her crotch. She came toward him on her hands and knees.

"Now you. Let me! I love to undress a man." She began by pulling off his boots, then his socks, and unbuckled his belt. Each move was a ceremony. When she got the buttons open on his fly she bent and kissed each one, then pushed the pants aside and kissed the bulge in his short drawers.

Pamela was panting now as she pulled his slacks down and off his feet, working on hands and knees, her generous breasts swaying and bouncing as she moved.

She gave a small cry and pushed him on his back on the blanket, kneeling over his crotch. Gently she began pulling down the short drawers, kissing them down from his waist. Soon she reached black, thick hair on his belly.

She looked up and threw a kiss to him, then pushed the drawers down more and more, kissing them off him. When she exposed the tip of his turgid penis, she screeched in delight, pushing the drawers down to reveal all of it.

Her eyes widened and she touched him tenderly, then kissed the rod from the pulsating purple tip to its roots. She lifted the length of it in her hand and shivered.

Then she lifted his erection and pushed it into her mouth. He thought she would never stop taking it in. She looked up at him and then bounced on him a few times before she squealed in delight and let him come out.

Quickly she slipped his drawers off and spread her five-foot nine-inch naked loveliness on top of him.

"George, lover George. You can have me just anyway you want. Upside down, standing up, any hole you can get into. But be sure to save enough for at least three times. I might just keep you here until it gets dark, making you fuck me again and again."

She shivered. "Everytime I say that word I just go all mushy. I mean it!"

"Stand up," Spur said, his voice going rough with his own desire. She stood and spread her beautiful legs. He bent and came to her probing.

"Never work," she said.

Just then he found the angle and slid into her well lubricated slot.

Pamela let out a wailing scream that could be heard for miles as he penetrated her and drove upward until he was locked to her. Her cry wailed out and she put her arms around him for support.

"Lift your legs and lock them behind my back," he said.

She stared at him a moment, then giggled, held tight with her arms and put her legs up.

"My God, it works!" she said softly. "I've never

. . . never fucked this way before!"

He caught her hips with his hands and pulled her away from him, then slammed her back. It was the only way they could get any action. The third time he did it, she crooned and then sobbed in a wild crying jag as her hips slammed against him and her whole body bucked and jolted in a series of grinding spasms.

Spur's legs gave way at last and he sat down on the blanket still in her. They fell over on their side and she brought her legs down and they rolled over with her on the bottom and both laughed. Then he stroked deeply into her and she groaned again. Three more plunges and she was off on another climax, shaking him with her this time until they both vibrated and her keening became a kind of wild song of pure physical pleasure, of sexual fulfillment and delicious rapture.

This time he kept pumping and when she finished her writhing and screeching, he came to the point of no return and slammed harder and harder at her. Now she was cheering him on. Urging him to drive harder and faster.

"Come on, lover, again, again! Drive it home, sink him deeper and deeper into me. That's the way, oh yes!"

He exploded at last and it caught them both in a driving frenzy as she climaxed again with him until they both sagged against the blanket, faces covered with sweat, a sheen of moisture over their bodies and they both panted and gasped for breath as they wound down from the physical and emotional high point.

She wrapped her arms and legs around him and wouldn't let him move.

"I want you inside of me until you shrivel into a

worm and fall out," she said when he could talk again. "It's never been that marvelous, never so fulfilling, so wonderful. This is no dewy eyed virgin talking. I say any fuck is a good fuck, but this was one that I'll remember as long as I can spread my legs for a man. Christ, but that was wonderful!"

They lay there for half an hour, bound together, talking about New York City. They had been to many of the same places. She grew up in a posh neighborhood, but not as fancy as his so he never told her. He said his father was a merchant in town, not letting her know the name of the stores which she would recognize.

At last they broke apart, kissed tenderly, and then she yelped and opened the picnic basket.

"We were so busy eating each other we forgot the food," she said. There was cold fried chicken and slabs of buttered bread. Fresh fruit and cheese and for dessert chocolate chip cookies. She had baked them herself. She shredded the chocolate into lumps and left it in the batter so it wouldn't all melt as it cooked.

She nibbled on his earlobe and breathed in his ear.

"Will that get you hard and sexy again?"

"Not until I get my strength back. I'm not sixteen you know."

Pamela laughed so hard she fell against him. Her creamy white breasts pushed at his chest but he straightened her.

"What's so funny?"

"Sixteen. When my brother was sixteen and I was fourteen, he dug a hole in the wall so he could spy on me in my room when I dressed. I knew the peep hole was there so I let him see only what I wanted to. When I felt real sexy I'd turn and give him a flash of a young breast.

"I was well developed for my age. What he forgot was that the hole worked both ways.

"I saw my first naked weenie that way. Then one night he got sexy and jacked off. Wow, I got to see him get hard and come and everything. Then later he had a friend over to stay the night and they got to bragging. It ended up they had a masturbating contest to see who could come the most times.

"I was amazed. I watched the whole thing. Six times each, then they just couldn't get their puds hard any more. It was a terrific sex lesson for me."

Spur chuckled. "No wonder you laughed about sixteen."

"The next day when I knew my brother was in his room, I made some noise so he knew I was there and I gave him a real show. I was feeling sexy then too, and I stripped down to bare ass for him and let him see me in front. It was an easy way of making it up to him for his show."

They both laughed and fondled each other. The food was gone. She jumped up and ran for the stream. It wasn't high then, maybe twenty feet wide and waist deep. He followed her and then splashed in the water and sat down, then dunked each other under the clear cold water.

"Fuck me under water!" she said.

"Can't be done."

"Can too."

"It's too cold, I can't even get him up."

"Stand," she said. She pulled his flaccid penis into her mouth and in only a few moments she had a mouthful. She floated on her back and he went between her legs and found the mark. They joined and she sank under water, then they moved closer to shore where she could hold the bottom and in a splashing thrashing time they made love again in the cool water.

Dripping and exhausted they ran to the blanket, moved it into the sun and let the rays warm them.

"The guns," she said suddenly. "Only two or three people in town know the facts. They are being provided by white men to the Indians, and the Indians agree to raid only certain areas, but they can use the guns to fight their traditional Indian foes wherever they find them."

"Who is giving the Indians the guns, Pam?"

She started to say something, then stopped. "No, I can't tell you. I would be killed if they found out." She grinned. "Did that sound dramatic enough?" She traced a fingernail down his chin, to his chest and down to his crotch.

"I'll tell you, next time. Like a continued story. I want at least one more roll in the grass with you before you fly out of here on a new assignment."

He looked up suddenly.

"Don't look so surprised. I figured out who you were the first day you came on the stage. You have government lawman written all over you. Then you got in that shootout and I lost track of you." She smiled. "Oh, that bullet wound in your shoulder is healing nicely. We wouldn't want to tell Tom Renshew about that, would we?"

"That could be the death of Mr. Renshew."

"We wouldn't want that to happen, either. Why don't we say right here, same time on Wednesday. That will give us both time to get our strength back."

"If I can make it. I do have a job to do."

"Of course, sweet George. And right now I'm part of that job you have to do." She stood on her knees and pushed one breast up to his face. He kissed it, then chewed on the nipple until it surged longer with hot blood.

"Thanks, she likes that. But, unfortunately, we have to get dressed now. Let me dress you. I enjoy that. I want to be the last one to see you covered up. Damn, what a man you are. I'm sorry you have to go. You can't believe how weird it is making love to a man shorter than I am. You're tall. I'm getting all of you I can while you're here."

It was half an hour later before they were dressed and back in the buggy. He drove her to the first screen of trees, then kissed her goodbye and she wheeled down the trail humming a sweet tune, and and remembering the best afternoon she had ever experienced in her thirty years.

Spur walked to his horse, rode cross country and came into town from the north. He had learned little. If Pamela knew about the guns, it was easy to figure that she had the word from her husband, the sheriff. Since he was under Renshew's thumb, it had to be Renshew who was running the guns.

He knew it. It tied in with what else he had picked up, but he couldn't prove it.

Spur went up to his room in the Far Northern Hotel. It was slightly after five o'clock. Virgin sat on the bed in a new conservative dress. She played solitaire and when she looked up, a smile broke over her face that was a pleasure to watch.

"Guess what?" she asked, bouncing up, scattering the set up of cards. She walked across the bed and reached for him, kissing his mouth. She frowned for a moment.

"Is that perfume?"

"I never wear perfume, it's probably some of yours."

"Whatever. You didn't guess what?"

"Your rich uncle in Philadelphia just died, and . . ."

She shook her head, her smile brighter. "I got a job! I'm going to be working as a helper and apprentice to Frances! Isn't that wonderful?"

Spur caught her around the hips. She still stood on the bed and was almost eye to eye with him. He kissed her cheek, then her lips softly.

"Virgin, that is great news. Frances is a fine lady."

"She's also letting me stay in back of the store with her and she's going to pay me . . . and everything!"

"Wonderful."

"And now you won't have to worry about me, or try to get me a job. And I'm a whore no more!"

"You never were a whore. You were just trying to get by. Did you ever wonder about married women? They put up with sex, let a man maul and use them when they don't want to. Why? For money, not cash but for room and board, for clothes, for trinkets and maybe jewels. And most of all, for security. Sure they bear the children, but that's just an aftermath of sex.

"Some people say that every woman is a whore, married or single, as long as she takes something for sex. That makes every man a pimp or a customer. That's why labels don't mean a damn thing. You were not a whore. You were simply a victim of your father's double standard. I'd still like to punch that man out if I could find him."

Virgin hugged him, then kissed his lips softly. Tears misted her eyes but she couldn't brush them away. "You're the kindest, sweetest, smartest man I've ever known. Will you marry me?"

He grinned. "We've been married in body for the past few days, but it can't last. We both know that. Now, you get yourself all fixed up pretty, and I'm going to take you to dinner in the dining room, and stare down anybody who tries to object. You'll be a smashing success.''

She was.

10

Clete Johnson and his band of rustlers moved toward the small valley where the thousand head of steers had been pastured by the Diamond D prior to driving them south.

Clete moved up by himself and checked the situation. Smoke came from the chimney in the line shack. The Diamond D riders were back on the job. Clete had left his horse well back, moving quickly from one patch of cover to the next. Now he watched the short fence holding the steers in. Chances are there would be a night rider.

Ten minutes later he spotted the rider coming out of the darkness. He rode slowly, making each trip along the fence last as long as he could.

Clete let the man ride past him, then the short man stood up and threw his five-inch-long hunting knife. Years of practice paid off. The heavy knife sailed straight and the sharp blade drove into the rider's back, slicing close to his spinal column and penetrating his lung. The Diamond D man fell forward on the saddle with a long wheeze.

The mount spooked, jolted in a fast turn and the rider tumbled off into the dirt. Clete moved up on him slowly, his six-gun ready. The cowboy tried to sit up, then attempted to call out, but before he could, fell backward again, he was dead.

Clete grinned and ran back to his horse. He brougth the other riders up, going around the small line shack. They'd take care of the other rider later.

Two of Clete's men started at each end of the short fence cutting the three strands of wire. They cut it off each post and let it fall in twenty foot ribbons on the ground.

When the way was clear, Clete brought his men around him.

"Listen good, you mavericks. This is where we make our money. We can't afford to let those steers stampede or we lose ninety percent of them. We get them up and head out a couple of old steers. When we get them moving, we drive them right over that line shack.

"That way we take care of the second guard and don't risk the sound of a shot. Let's get the cattle moving. They won't want to go. We roust them, kick them, slap them with ropes. Anything to get them up and moving. Let's do it!"

Cattle used to resting all night are hard to move. Before long half the cowboys were on the ground, kicking and swearing at the beef, slapping them with knotted ropes, twisting tails.

Gradually they got a section near the far side moving and they stumbled into the still down critters, urging them up. It took them an hour to get the herd on its feet and moving toward the line shack.

By then they had made so much noise the second guard woke up and came out shooting. Clete fired twice at him, then used his rifle trailing the man on foot as he ran across the prairie.

When Clete came back from his shootout with the guard, he figured they had the whole herd on the move. Two men rode on the sides, keeping the steers moving generally toward the south. Here they headed down an open valley and toward a far river where they would be off Diamond D land.

The critters moved slowly, some tried to lay down and had to be prodded with rifle barrels. Slowly the herd picked up the idea and the cattle walked forward, maybe three miles an hour. Clete remembered that on many a cattle drive, ten miles a day was a good move. All he wanted to do was put the steers on a fourteen hour march and get them well off the Diamond D land.

Now he was worried about the head start. He swore at himself for not making sure of the other guard. He thought he'd nailed him with a rifle slug, but he wasn't sure. At least the man was walking. It would take him half the night to get back to the Diamond D ranch. If he was shot up badly enough, he might not make it at all.

Clete rode around the herd. It looked like more than a thousand to him now after slapping at least half of them on the hind quarters with a rope to keep them moving. Clete had an idea they were going to earn their money by the time they got this herd pushed down as far as the railroad in Kansas.

Clete circled the herd again, helped the lead man angle them more to the southeast and then went back to help punch in strays and some of the laggards. Every steer they lost was twenty to thirty dollars out of pocket, depending on the market.

When the herd moved along well for half an hour, Clete told the tail-end-charlie herder he was going to follow their back trail for a half mile and check it out. He rode at an easy canter, pleased with the start of the operation. He'd be a lot happier when they were fifty miles away, and the Diamond D brands had all been worked over into two new brands. But that would have to wait until they had time.

He rode back two miles, to a point just past the line shack. For half an hour he sat on the ground and listened to the night sounds. Nowhere did he hear any movement, nor any sign of a man moving across the prairie.

Clete mounted up and rode back to the herd. With any luck at all that second guard was bleeding to death out there somewhere, and they had their head start! He had to get the men to move the herd a little faster. Every mile now meant that much more safety tomorrow.

As Clete rode off, Kirk Olson lifted up from behind a scrub crab apple tree some homesteader had planted. The man swore softly at the rider, then checked the big red handkerchief that he held over a bullet wound in his side. He wasn't sure how bad it was.

He knew for damn sure that it wasn't good. The awful fact came through as well that he was over eight miles from the house ranch, and he had to make it on his own two feet.

Kirk Olson pushed himself up and began to walk. There wasn't one fucking thing in the world he hated to do more than walk. If he had to go from the barn to the well, he'd saddle up and ride, even if it was only a hundred yards. A cowboy was a man on a horse!

He cursed openly now into the soft night air for

ever leaving the line shack without his horse. He had seen old blaze swept away as the steers came rushing by. Once free of the cattle, the cow pony would head for the home ranch. He could be half way there by now. That by itself might alert them.

The second thing he most hated in the world was rustlers. They were lower than men. They had no right to live. He'd gladly hang every one he could catch in the act. No court needed. Just the judge, jury and executioner of a good strong rope!

Step after step. He checked his side again. Blood was still coming. He held the handkerchief against the spot. There were two wounds, one where the slug cut into him, and another where it came out. Another three inches to the right and he'd be buzzard bait.

He still might be when he told Tom Renshew the bad news. The old man would go into a rage. Kirk figured he'd find the foreman and tell him.

As he walked he slanted north and then to the right. A good eight miles. How far had he come? Maybe a quarter of a mile. There was one small stream where he could get a drink and maybe wash off his side. At least it wasn't hot.

Kirk Olson swore again and plodded on. After this he'd never walk another ten feet if his life depended on it.

By midnight, Clete was satisfied with their progress. They had struck shortly after eight P.M. It was barely dark when he walked up on the herd. Now they had been moving the critters for more than three hours at a good steady pace. They should be nine miles south, or thereabouts.

He wasn't sure of a night drive, but the darkness seemed to keep the animals bunched more, as if they were bedded down but still moving. They seemed easier to handle at night in the cool air than the same steers would when daylight came.

Clete circled the steers, urging his men to keep them moving quickly, just short of a trot. They couldn't risk a stampede.

He scanned the sky. A few clouds, a quarter moon. No chance of a thunderstorm or lightning. He'd seen many a lightning storm scatter a herd of cattle over half a Texas county. So far, so good.

Clete tried to decide what he would do with his half of the money. Nobody had argued when he laid out the shares. It had been his plan, he was the leader, he took most of the profits. He could have nearly ten thousand if it worked right.

Damn! With that much money he could go back home and buy a business and get somebody else to run it for him and sit on his ass and find a pretty little woman to fuck day and night. Even that would get tiresome after a while.

A ranch of his own? Not much for ten thousand. A homestead, maybe, and a good woman and six boys to help run it. But then he would have to worry about rustlers. Clete laughed. He would earn the money first, then spend it.

Kirk Olson wiped sweat off his forehead with a grimy cotton shirt sleeve. He checked the cowboy's Waterbury, the Big Dipper. It was partly covered by a cloud but he could get its position by the pointer stars that showed where the North Star was. The time was a little before midnight.

He slumped on the grass and rubbed his legs. Kirk thought he was as tough as old boot leather, but the way he hurt he decided riding and walking used far different muscles.

Could he walk three miles an hour? That was a mile in twenty minutes. At once he knew he hadn't been moving that fast. His side hurt more now. He realized his steps were shorter. Each time he moved his left leg, his side stabbed pain at him. He would think about something else.

Two and a half miles an hour. Three hours would give him almost seven miles. No, he hadn't started right away. Then the bastard came back to gloat and watch for him and that cost him another half hour.

Maybe he had been walking for two hours. Maybe five miles, more likely three and a half or four. The problem was he was going slower and slower.

Daylight!

He might not find the ranch before daylight. Then the men would have a long ride.

The more he thought about it, the less he worried. Those steers might not go more than three or four miles before they refused to move and simply bedded down. He had tried to night drive a small herd once. In the end he gave up and waited until morning.

Even if they got ten miles away, they would have to stop and rest. Twenty Diamond D riders could cover fifteen, eighteen miles in a hurry. They could each take two horses and do eight miles an hour if they had to.

Tom would find the raiders before noon, if he could walk into the ranch by sunup.

Kirk sighed, stood, held the handkerchief to his side and began walking. He had stopped bleeding. The handkerchief was glued to his side where the blood dried. Now he had to hold it there.

Another step.

One more step.

Kirk Olson willed himself to keep walking.

It was either keep walking or die out here on the prairie.

About one o'clock he came to the creek. He pulled the handkerchief free of his side and saw in the faint moonlight that it bled very little. He washed out the cloth in the small stream, drank his fill, then took off his boots and washed his feet and dusted out his socks. When his feet dried he put on the socks again, pulled on his boots, and continued walking over the wild, Dakota prairie.

He knew this place. The route was more familiar now. He was a little over three miles from the ranch. With any luck he would make it well before daylight.

Tom Renshew stood at his bedroom door, a lighted lamp in his hand as he talked to his foreman. He had been mad as hell when the man knocked on his door. Now he nodded.

"Get together twenty men, the best rifle shots we have. I'll be down to the corral in five minutes. Every man needs at least fifty rounds in his saddle bags. If they don't have ammunition, dig some out of the box you have under the bunk. We'll make an example of these bastards they'll talk about all over Dakota for years."

They rode out twenty minutes later. It was just after four-thirty A.M. and would be getting light in an hour. Kirk Olson had not been berated by the foreman or the owner. He was treated by their resident first aid man and put to bed.

The riders were sleepy, mad, curious, but nobody asked a question. They each had one horse and they pushed them at five miles an hour, loping for a half mile, then walking a half mile.

That way they could eat up ten miles in two hours and still have good mounts under them.

They did not ride back to the line shack. Instead

they angled across country in the only direction the rustlers could take. They would try for the end of the Souris Bluffs where they could slip across the river and continue on south.

After an hour's hard ride, Renshew called a halt and told the men where they were going and what had happened.

"We know how to deal with rustlers. And this is a thousand head we're talking about. There could be a fight. We want as many of them alive as possible. Does everyone understand that?"

When they passed the ten mile point, Renshew sent a scout riding out front. He cut the trail of the herd a half mile over and reported it. They swung over and followed the cut up prairie, where four thousand hooves had chopped up the sod.

The scout came back an hour later. It was fully light now and nearing eight A.M. They had brought no food. It would be a fight and run mission. They understood that.

Renshew listened to his scout and nodded.

"Far as I can tell they're stopped just below that next creek we call the Crooked. Looks like the critters just played out on them. Most of the beef are bedded down along the creek and they got their bellies full of water. Don't look like they're moving anymore for three or four hours at the least."

"How far ahead?"

"Three miles, no more."

"I know the spot. No way to sneak up on them. We don't want to wait until dark. We split up." For a moment Tom wished he'd brought his son, Harry, along. It would have been good training for him. But he knew Harry would not have been able to stand up to the pressure. He looked back at his foreman.

"Jed, you take half the men and swing wide and

come up the river from downstream. We'll both try to be in position by ten o'clock. Then we simply ride in shooting. Remember to shoot low and knock them down without killing them. That's damn important this time.''

The foreman nodded and hurried away.

Tom Renshew had not been in the war, but he knew about tactics. He looked at his watch. Five minutes to go. He checked his men. They had moved up to within two hundred yards of the rustlers and the steers. He and his ten men would ride hard at the outlaws, shoot them out of the saddle and capture those not wounded.

Far on the other side of the slight depression near the river he thought he saw movement. A horse burst out of the brush and then ten men galloped forward. That was Jed and the rest of the men!

"Charge!" Renshew bellowed, and he swept forward with his men. Twenty guns fired from horseback at the four rustlers near the noon time fire. One rustler went down with a slug in his arm. The other three tried to get to their horses, but they were cut off.

More hot lead thundered in at them and three threw up their hands. Five men from each group raced around and bedded down steers, searching for any outriders. They chased two back into the camp where they were captured, and a third one was shot through the head and brought in draped over his saddle.

The beef, bone weary from the long night-time walk, hardly noticed the commotion. Most dozed through it and they stayed in place.

Jed assigned two men to ride herd on the critters and the others prodded the rustlers into a line sitting in the grass, staring up at Tom Renshew who positioned himself so the men had to look into the sun to see him.

"Who is your leader?" he barked.

Nobody said a word.

Tom walked up to a man sitting with his legs spread, his arms folded and a scowl on his face. Renshew kicked him in the crotch, bowling him over and into the dirt where he wailed in agony.

"Which of you is the boss of this outfit?" he asked again.

One man looked up, his face blanched white. Sweat popped on his forehead. His hands shook. He pointed at the man beside him.

"He is. That's Clete Johnson, all his idea. I never wanted to do it anyhow!"

Two men grabbed the rustler said to be the leader and stood him up. They held him on each side by his arms.

Renshew stood in front of him. "You the ring-leader here?"

Clete looked away.

Renshew punched him in the face, his big fist splattering Clete's nose. Blood gushed out.

"God damn!" Clete bellowed.

"So you can talk. You're the ramrod in this rustling gang?"

"Would it matter?" Clete said evenly.

"Not a hell of a lot. Are you?"

"Hell yes. What can you do but kill me?"

Tom motioned two more of his men up. One held his legs while the other opened his belt and pulled down his pants. His privates hung in the breeze.

"Clete Johnson, you're a slimy bastard, do you know that?"

Johnson looked away.

One man held each of Johnson's legs and spread

them. Before Clete knew what was going to happen, Renshew bent, grabbed his scrotum and testicles, pulled them down and slashed with his sharp pocket knife just above his hand severing the scrotum.

Johnson howled in terrible pain, then collapsed. They threw a bucket of water on him. When he came back to consciousness he lay in the grass, his hands holding his injured genitals.

Renshew looked down at him. "I should make you live like that, make you suffer, but that wouldn't be fair. Get up, you're first."

They lifted him to his feet. He had bitten through his lip leaving bleeding teeth marks. Two men hoisted him on a horse with no saddle. The biggest tree was an old maple. A rope snaked over it and a second rider placed the nose around Clete's neck and pulled it tight. The long end had been tied off around the trunk.

"Clete Johnson, I sentence you to die for the crime of rustling, and for killing Willy Grand, the other herder." He nodded. Someone dug a sharp spur over the hind quarters of the black horse and it snorted and jolted ahead.

Johnson slid off the horse's rump, dropped to the end of the rope and his neck snapped.

One by one they hung the six men. Three of them were crying uncontrollably. Four of them could not control their bladders. The last one had watched with mounting horror as the five men he had ridden with kicked and twitched as they died at the end of the ropes.

He screamed and bellowed with rage. He was the youngest, a kid not more than eighteen. His hands had been tied behind his back and he butted Tom Renshew and bit him on the hand. The rancher shook his head at the man tying the last hangman's knot.

Renshew took out his .44 and when the kid ran at him again, Renshew shot him three times in the head. When he fell, Renshew stepped over his body and fired once more through the back of his head.

The rancher stared for a minute at the seven bodies, two shot and five hung.

He knew the word would get around. It would be one hell of a long time before anybody tried to rustle stock from the Diamond D again.

He gave a sigh. He wished like hell that Ed was still around. He'd be happy to turn the ranch over to younger hands. He looked at the dead men once more, then got on his horse and rode back toward the ranch. The twenty men followed him. It was a silent ride back to the Diamond D ranch headquarters. There was nothing to say. The cowboys realized they had witnessed a bit of history made. It was an act of vigilante justice that they might never see again. Each of them would remember it for the rest of his life.

11

Spur and Virgin had breakfast together at the hotel, then she hurried down the street to Frances's dress shop. She would move in there as soon as they could find a small bed.

Spur had uneasy stirrings. He knew he should be doing more about the problem of Renshew and the Indians. He had talked to Virgin about it but she wasn't sure where the Yanktonai Indians had their summer camp.

He had to go up there and talk to their chief. If the problem were only a few renegades, he would leave it up to the Indian justice system. He had to go make the effort.

He went to the court house and talked to one of the clerks who was older than the rest. He told her with all confidence who he was and why he was in town. He pledged her not to tell anyone.

She nodded and smiled with a new self-importance. Then he asked her where the Indians had their camps. She had been working on some land grants and other land matters, and had a good idea

132

of the potential points high along the Canadian border.

She pinpointed them for him on a small map and gave it to him. She said this was the best information anyone in the county might have on the whereabouts of the summer camp. He swore her to secrecy again and headed for the general store. He was going to need some gear.

An hour later he had his equipment and a good horse from the livery. He had a twenty-five mile ride ahead of him, and he wasn't sure how much of it he would be allowed to make alone, and unchallenged.

If the Yanktonai had any kind of lookout system at all, he would be picked up shortly after he entered their home lands, and shadowed all the way to wherever they decided they should stop for a talk.

He would be going openly, riding with a white flag for all to see. The Yanktonai would honor it, from what he had heard about them. Most lived on a reservation in unclaimed lands, and their chief, Many Winters, had met with Indian Department people twice.

Spur knew exactly what to buy at the store. More and more of his background came flittering back to him. He had to reach for it, but it was there. Now he could remember that he grew up in New York City, went to good schools, then graduated from Harvard University in Cambridge.

Later he worked for two years in his father's stores, then when the war came he was commissioned in the army and served a year in the front lines. He reached the rank of captain and was in command of a company before he was brought to Washington D.C. by the New York Senator who was a good family friend.

He served as military advisor to the Senator until

the end of the war.

When the Secret Service was formed in 1865, he applied for it and was appointed one of the original agents. In those days the Secret Service had as its sole responsibility protecting the currency from counterfeiting.

He served six months in Washington, then was appointed as agent in charge of the new St. Louis office. There he was responsible for the states and territories west of the Mississippi.

By that time the Secret Service was the only police agency with the power to enforce Federal regulations or to apprehend criminals who had crossed state lines. The workload and the variety of problems expanded tremendously.

Spur rode along the Souris River where it meandered northward. It was a little over sixty miles to the Canadian border, but he was sure he would not have to go that far to find the Indians.

He rode all the first day, making good time. When he at last found a camping place near the river in a flurry of small trees and brush, he figured he had covered a little over twenty miles. So far he had seen no Indians, no smokes, and no sign that the Indian tribe used the area for hunting.

He remembered more now as his memory came back a little at a time. He knew about lots of the cases he had worked on, the people, the Indians, the killers. Maybe that bash on the head in the mob the other day had helped.

Spur made a cold camp. Any smoke in this area would be like a dagger aimed at his heart. The Indians could smell a smoke in an unoccupied land for ten miles. He didn't want them to think he was a tenderfoot.

Tomorrow morning he would make a fire, have a

good meal of flapjacks, bacon, coffee and hashbrown potatoes. By then he would be ready to invite the Yanktonai to come and parley with him. He had a feeling he was getting close to their territory.

As a precaution, he took his blankets and wormed his way thirty feet into nearly impenetrable brush. Even an Indian would make a wagon load of noise trying to sneak in there. It would be enough to wake Spur.

He grinned as he settled down in his blankets. The old ways were coming back. He knew who he was and why he was out here in this Park-Avenue-forsaken place. And he was glad he was here. For the first time in many nights Spur McCoy was at peace with himself and the life he had chosen.

He slept like a newborn foal.

By mid morning he had worked around a lake that fed and was fed by the Souris River. Upstream he began finding signs that Indians had used the area. A broken shard of pottery. A sharpened rock that had probably been used to scrape buffalo hides. Near a deep pool in a bend in the river he found footprints in the mud along the bank, as if a dozen young Indians had used the old swimming hole.

That morning he had cut a six foot long willow, trimmed off the leaves and tied a white handkerchief to the tip of it. The large end he wedged into his saddle, and tied it securely to the boot that held his Spencer.

He was officially under the white flag of truce. Every Indian nation in the West recognized the flag. Whether the Yanktonai chose to abide by it could be another matter.

Before eleven o'clock he had that creepy feeling along the back of his neck that spelled danger. He knew at once that the Indians had spotted him, and were shadowing him, perhaps passing him along from one lookout to the next.

He scanned the ridges, but found no smoke signals. Nor did he see any flashes of the sun off metal or bright copper bells some Indians wore on their finery.

Still there was more evidence of Indians. A large dead tree had been chopped down and split open. It contained a swarm of the white man's flies, and he saw honey oozing out through a great crack in the tree. The bees were restoring their hive and storing up for the winter.

A quarter of a mile farther on a doe deer herded two fawns across the shallow reaches of the Souris. She pushed them into the water which was only knee deep on them, and butted them to hurry across.

Half way into the water she saw Spur. She only flipped her tail and hurried the twins across and into the brush. A moment later he saw the three bounding over an open area heading for the higher ridges. Something had been chasing her. Otherwise the mothering instinct would never have let her push her offspring so close to a white man.

An owl hooted to his left. Spur's head snapped around. This was not the time of day for owls. An Indian wearing only a breechcloth and holding his hunting bow and three arrows in his right hand sat bareback on a war pony. When the brave was sure that Spur saw him, he faded into the brush.

They wanted him to know they knew he was there. Now the option was his, to continue, or to turn back.

He rode forward quickly, so there would be no doubt in their minds.

Two miles ahead, and just before noon, Spur broke out of a woodsy, timbered spot along the river and came to a meadow half a mile square. Far to the left he could see a grazing band of buffalo. He guessed there were no more than fifty to seventy-five. They must have broken off from some herd.

The waist high grass would last the buffs half the summer.

He heard the owl call again and ahead of him less than fifty yards, three braves rode out of trees next to the river on sturdy black mounts he figured had to be ex-U.S. Cavalry horseflesh. The brave in the center wore a headdress with feathers cascading down his back and over the flank of the horse.

Spur stopped.

The three Indians stopped.

Then the center rider touched the horse with his knees and it walked slowly forward.

Spur took the white flag and held it high as he walked his horse toward the Indian.

As he came closer to the Indian, Spur saw that he man was probably in his fifties—an old man for an Indian. His face was not painted for war. His war bonnet, the long trailing feather headdress, was as much for ceremony now as for war. The two men stopped their horses when they were a dozen feet apart.

Spur held up the white flag, then positioned it again in the boot, and made the sign for FRIEND. He held his right hand in front of his chin with his palm out and two small fingers bent down and held with his thumb. He raised his hand in front of his eyes.

The Yanktonai chief did the same. Spur slid off his horse, took out his six-gun with finger and thumb on the butt and placed it in his saddle bag. Then he sat down on the grass his legs crossed and waited for the old brave.

The Chief moved slowly, slid off his horse and

took a knife from his breechcloth band and dropped it at his horse's feet. Then he frowned and sat down facing Spur.

The old Indian signed slowly, watching the round-eye's reaction. WHITE MAN COME YANK-TONAI HUNTING GROUNDS.

Spur read the signs, nodded his understanding. Then replied with signs of his own:

YES. BAD PROBLEM WHITE CAMP. YANK-TONAI RENEGADES RAID WHITE SETTLERS.

The old chief read the signs, and anger flickered in his eyes, then despair came.

He clasped all but one pointing finger and motioned with it from upright to the ground. YES. Then he stopped. YOUNG BUCKS. HARD TO CONTROL. COME.

They both stood. The chief held up one finger and swept his hand toward his own face. Spur should go with him.

Both men put their weapons back in place. The old Indian tried twice before he mounted his war pony. Spur looked at his horse's foot, staring the other way until he was sure the chief was mounted. Then he stepped into the saddle, and keeping both hands in sight, rode up to the chief, who turned, and they rode on toward the north.

When they came to the other two Indians on horseback, the braves fell in on both sides of the pair as they moved foward. Spur did not feel threatened. The Indian beside him appeared to be in his late twenties, a seasoned warrior. Most of the Indians became warriors when they were fourteen or fifteen.

He watched the countryside come alive as they rode. Just past the next line of brush, he saw a dozen squaws picking berries along the stream. Others dug for roots.

A dozen young boys eight or ten scampered through the brush playing Indian, attacking each other, whooping in delight when they subdued a foe, then rushing off to a new battle.

Ahead a half mile he saw smoke. The camp as they came into it was not on alert. Everyone went about his or her usual work projects.

Six women worked over fresh buffalo hides, laboriously scraping the meat side with sharpened stones, cutting away all of the meat and fat, leaving the hide as thick as possible, with no dents or gouges in it.

Other women worked on the hair side of skins, scraping off the thick buffalo hair. The women looked up curious, then ducked their heads and went back to scraping.

One of the women did not duck down. She had been pretty once, but now her nose had been slit two or three times. It had not healed properly and disfigured her good looks. Another slice showed on her cheek. They were traditional forms of punishment for women caught in adultery by their husbands. She watched Spur until he was out of sight.

The tipis were larger than Spur had remembered. Some were fifteen feet in diameter, the long poles rising twenty feet in the air where they were braced together. They were covered mostly by tanned buffalo hides carefully sewn together.

A group of laughing little girls ran by, barely noticing the riders. All wore only breechclothes, black hair flying, breasts not yet budding. Then Spur looked again. One of them was different. She had long blonde hair that had been bleached nearly white in the sun. She was laughing and teasing her friends, sturdy moccasins on her feet. When she glanced at him he saw sparkling blue eyes.

Spur steeled himself not to shout or even to stare at the girl. He looked beyond her, then to the other side. What in blazes did it mean? Had she been kidnapped from some family? Was she the result of a raid on a white settlement? Spur felt a driving, unquenchable need to know. However it was not the sort of question he could ask the chief.

They wound through the camp of some sixty tipis. Quickly Spur guessed there could be fifty warriors in the band. That could leave half a dozen or so of the young bucks who would be hard to keep track of —or control. Their hunting jaunts could turn into raids.

The horses stopped in front of a large tipi. Three wives lined up outside the chief's tent. One caught the hair-braided hackamore controlling the mount. A second hurried forward and accepted the headdress when he took it off. The third wife was the youngest. She seemed little more than thirteen, but her belly was fat with child.

They walked into the tent with the chief leading. He went to the right, circling the open space between the fire in the center and the robes and heaps of goods and belongings next to the outside of the tipi. Then the old chief sat down on a polished rock and stared at the small cooking fire.

He called a young brave who came into the tipi, moved around to the right and then sat beside the chief. The old man chattered with the buck for a moment, then watched Spur.

The young brave was Dog Piss. He stared at Spur with curiosity, then let the strong-medicine white man's gold piece swing out from the rawhide thong around his neck. He saw the white man look at it. The roundeye did not betray any emotion.

"White chief is brave man come to Yanktonai camp. Chief Many Winters show you this is not war camp. We live in peace. Chief say white man kill grass from Mother Earth. Tear up her land, kill sod, try to plant new grass. Not good. Chief Many Winters say, Yanktonai stay in hunting grounds, roundeyes stay in their lodges, all will be fine."

Spur felt the relief of being able to communicate through an English-speaking Indian. He had a better idea for the old chief. "Tell Chief Many Winters I understand. I try to keep roundeyes out of Yanktonai hunting grounds. But still wild young braves raid roundeye settlers, kill, steal horses. The young braves are raiding in exchange for new fires-many-times-rifles."

When the translation was made, Spur was not sure the old chief was told correctly. He didn't seem upset enough.

Spur looked at the chief, made the sign for GUN, then signed the working of a rifle lever to indicate a rifle. He hurried on signing, MANY RIFLES TO YOUNG BRAVES FOR RAIDING.

The old chief said something sharply to his interpreter who started to argue, then backed away and left the tipi.

Now the old chief looked sad but more interested. He signed the words HOW MANY. Spur answered with the number of THIRTY or FORTY.

The old chief looked away. He controlled his face with an effort. At last he faced Spur and signed slowly so there would be no mistake.

I WILL FIND RIFLES IF THEY ARE HERE. WE LIVE IN PEACE.

Spur nodded that he understood, signed, I MUST GO, and they rose together.

Outside Spur's horse was rushed up to him by one

of the chief's three wives. He mounted and the two escorts who had brought him in came beside him and began the ride downstream.

At a field just outside the last tent, a dozen braves cavorted in a horse riding contest. They were competing against each other.

One brave came riding across the grass completely hidden on the far side of his mount except for one leg which caught the cinch strap across the pony's back.

Another brave galloped across the grass, guiding the pony only with his knees weaving between posts set in the ground and hitting targets with arrows as he flashed by them at twenty yards.

Braves mounted racing horses, tumbled off galloping mounts and caught hold of twenty foot long reins, designed to help pull them away from a rampaging herd of buffalo if they fell off during a hunt.

A dozen other skills of the Indian rider were demonstrated. The escorts had stopped when Spur did to watch the show. When it was over Spur waved to them and then rode south with the scouts.

Spur wanted to give them something. He fished in his pants and came up with a three bladed folding pocket knife. He had heard of the Indian's love of gambling. He showed them the pocket knife and pointed to each, then pretended to break it in half and give each half.

They laughed. He took out a coin and showed them head and tails. They didn't understand. He signed the word CONTEST and PRIZE to them. Then he used the knife to carve a one inch wide bare spot on a tree. He pointed to his knife, then to each of them and made a throwing motion.

At last they understood. He signed ONE TRY,

and they nodded. Both braves watched him. He paced off ten steps, about twenty yards and drew a mark on the grass with his boot. Then he pointed to each of them and motioned for them to throw.

When they understood they vied for the right to go first. Spur pointed at one, and he toed the mark, whipped back his hand and threw a six inch hunting knife he must have captured. The blade flew straight, hit the tree but was a foot below the mark.

The second Indian threw and the edge of his blade touched the mark on the tree.

Spur made a little ceremony of giving the winner the folding knife and they signed that they must return. He waved to them and rode away, not sure what he had learned, but he knew the rifles in the Indian camp had been a big surprise to Chief Many Winters.

He wondered about the nine year old white girl. Who was she? Hadn't she been missed? What could he possibly do about rescuing her?

12

Tom Renshew rode silently between his two best enforcers. It was two days after the rustler hangings. The town had quieted down a little after the first outburst of both protest and support for his vigilante efforts out on the prairie. Now there was something else he had to do. It had been building for some time and couldn't wait another day.

The man was becoming a problem. He was an important part of the life of their little town and rather than just killing him, Tom had figured out a different method that he knew would work. It had before.

He was disturbed that nothing had been found of the killer who had cut down Edward. His son's death was still unresolved and there had been no blood vengeance. That was his second priority. First came Ray Krause.

For months the man had been stirring up trouble, starting ugly rumors about the Diamond D and its operation as well as the owners themselves. Tom decided it was high time to stop the talk once and for all before the man's big mouth got everyone in trouble.

The letter to the Attorney General had been the capper. How the store owner could come up with such innuendoes without actually saying anything he could be charged with was upsetting to Tom. The letter had suggested and hinted and alluded to wrongdoing on a rather grand scale by Tom Renshew. In one or two of the wild claims he had come too close to the truth, and Tom wanted to teach this man such a lesson that he would be no more threat.

He had just the right form of persuasion in mind.

One of the men with Tom left the other two at Main Street and took the three horses up the alley. Tom gave him three minutes on his gold filled pocket watch, then walked into Ray Krause's Hardware and Farm and Ranch Supplies store. There was one customer. Renshew and his man, Red, prowled around the front of the store until the customer left, then Red went to the front door, locked it, turned the sign over to read, "Closed," and pulled down the window shade.

Red sauntered to the back, as Ray came around the counter.

"Yes, sir, Mr. Renshew. What can I get for you today?"

"A little respect." Renshew said. His fist came flashing out, caught Ray on the jaw and drove him back a step.

"What in hell?"

"You just closed up for the day, Ray. Let's go out the back door."

"You ain't wearing a gun, Renshew. I could beat you to my six shooter under the counter."

"Not and stay alive," a voice said from the hardware store's back room.

Ray looked over and saw a sawed off shotgun's double barrels aimed directly at him.

"Just what do you want from me, Renshew?"

"I told you, a little respect. Let's move."

Five minutes later they walked into the back door of Ray Krause's house two blocks over from the store and a block off Main Street. It was a comfortable house, with two stories and an attic.

Ida Krause looked up from her cross stitching. She had seldom known her husband to be home during business hours. She watched, startled, worried now as he walked into the parlor.

He saw her concern and held up his hand. "Ida, don't get upset. I just needed to come home for a bit. I brought some company with me."

Ida stood at once and touched her hair. Ida was not a pretty woman. She was sturdy, solid, thirty-four with mousy brown hair and more than a hundred and forty pounds on her five foot two inch frame.

"Goodness, company?"

Renshew walked in from the kitchen, followed by Red and the second enforcer he called Wyoming. Red had his six-gun out and aimed at Ray.

Renshew doffed his brown hat. "Mrs. Krause. Nice to meet you. I was wondering if you would be so kind as to show me the upstairs bedrooms."

Ida Krause jolted back a half step. What an unusual request. She looked at her husband who nodded.

"Yes, of course, right this way."

They went up the stairs, Wyoming first, then Ida with her husband close behind her and Tom bringing up the rear. In the first bedroom they saw that it was obviously the children's room. Two children were in school.

The second room was the master bedroom, containing all of the parents' things.

Wyoming had carried a thin roll of heavy twine with him. He caught up a straight chair, pushed Ray Krause into it and began tying him securely to the chair.

"What on earth is going on here?" Ida asked, her fists on her ample hips.

"Ida, your husband is going to be taught a small lesson. If he learns it, he will live. If he doesn't, both of you will die long before the children get home from school."

She looked at Ray who could only stare back at her.

"Whatever do you mean?"

"Your husband has been telling lies about me, Ida. He's going to stop. You're going to help him."

"How can I help him? I don't . . ."

Ida Krause shivered. She bolted for the door, but Red caught her roughly from the back, his arms circling her, both hands gripping tightly her heavy breasts. He grinned and held her.

"You can let her go, Red," Renshew said.

"You just can't do this!" Ida shrilled her voice rising. "We have laws . . ."

"I own the law in this county."

"You'll never get away with it. People saw you."

"None who will talk. Ida, you have a simple decision to make. Ray Krause gets killed, right here in front of your eyes, unless you agree to strip your clothes and play all of the strange little sexual games we want you to. Do you understand what I'm saying?"

"I don't believe you," Ida said softly. "You couldn't do that."

Renshew nodded and Red put away his revolver, took out a four inch knife and made a thin slice across Ray's forehead. Ray choked back a scream. Blood beaded in the slice, then began to run down his forehead in red streaks.

"Ida, it isn't pretty, is it, watching a man bleed? The next slice will be across his throat, venting both his carotid arteries, and your husband will gush out his life's blood in about ten seconds. Right now he's thirty seconds away from being dead. How do you feel?"

Ida swayed. Tom moved to catch her, but she kept her feet.

She shook her head. "You mean . . ." She swallowed. "You want me to take my clothes off and be a whore for you, and you'll let Ray go and it all will be fine?"

"Just like peaches and cream, Ida. Ray will learn his lesson. He'll stop making up stories about me. We need him here in town with his store. Everything will be just like it was before today, except Ray won't tell those wild stories about me."

"Don't do it, Ida. I won't sit here and watch him rape you. NO! I'd rather be dead first!"

"Men get so emotional at times like this," Renshew said. "Ida, you're the level-headed one. Which would be less painful for you, to get fucked a few times, or to be a widow?"

Slowly Ida began to unbutton the thin everyday dress she wore. It came free to the waist, then she grabbed it by the skirt and lifted it over her head. She stared straight ahead. A moment later she lifted off two petticoats. She looked at her husband, her face flushed with concern.

"Ray, I don't want you to die. This won't hurt me. You know a man can't use up a woman. Learn the lesson, Ray. He might be touching me, and inside me, but I'll never feel him."

Renshew slapped her to stop her talking. His knife

snipped straps over her shoulders and he pulled
away the chemise and wrapper so her big breasts
billowed out.

"Look at them tits!" Red chortled. "Hey, do I get
a turn?"

Renshew looked at Ray. "Why not, she's free and
looks sturdy."

His knife sliced down each side of the knee length
drawers Ida wore, then she was naked. Renshew
pushed her toward the bed, made her get on her
hands and knees so her breasts hung down.

Red and Wyoming picked up Ray's chair and
moved the tied-up man up close to the bed for better
viewing.

Renshew moved the point of his knife within a
quarter of an inch from Ray's eyeball. "You will
keep your eyes open at all times and watch us on the
bed. Anytime you don't watch, your woman will get
a three inch slice. First on her forehead, then on each
cheek, then her tits and her arms. You want her cut
up?"

Ray Krause shook his head. "God no! I'll watch!"

Renshew stepped back, pocketed the knife, slid
out of his pants and his underwear and jumped on
the bed behind the woman. He was hard already, he
went up behind her where she had remained on her
hands and knees. He adjusted her, then rammed
forward.

"Oh, no!" the woman shrieked. "Not down there!
That's wicked, unnatural!"

"Shut up!" Renshew roared. "I'll take you
anywhere I want to as many times as I want to." He
leaned around her, grabbed her hanging breasts and
mauled them. Quickly he climaxed. Renshew
grunted, pulled away from her and called over
Wyoming.

"Your turn, Wyoming. Just so you leave some for

me. I need ten minutes to recover."

For two hours the three men took turns with Ida, battering her, assaulting her everywhere possible, forcing her to do strange and unnatural things she had never even heard about.

Twice Ray had looked away in shame and fury. Twice Wyoming's blade had sliced Ida, both times on the forehead. The cuts would leave scars unless treated promptly.

Silent tears rolled down Ray's face. He had never been caught in such a position before. Someone else suffered because of him and there was nothing he could do about it.

Slowly the rage built in him. He would agree to anything now. But as soon as he was free he would get a good rifle and he would lay in wait, and he would blow Tom Renshew straight into hell! It had to be. There was no other way to deal with an animal like this.

The three men dressed.

Ida lay on the bed, her body battered and her forehead bloody. She twitched, her eyes closed, waiting the next disgusting assault. She had not broken. She had not cried. She had not screamed at them. She was sturdy German stock. She would take the punishment, and she would kill all three of them later. She would find a time. Make a time!

When she heard the men dressing, she opened her eyes.

"You may dress now as well, if you wish, Ida. Or you can lay around naked all day like a whore." She rolled to the far side of the bed and quickly dressed in clothes grabbed from her dresser.

Renshew stood in front of Ray.

"A little lesson for you, Mr. Krause. Never say a bad word against a Renshew or the Diamond D. You should have learned that by now." He motioned the men into the hall.

"Oh, one last suggestion. Don't get any wild ideas about revenge. I've told three of my men at the ranch about this lesson for you. They have written instructions that if anything at all happens to me, like an accident, or being bushwhacked or suddenly finding poison in my gravy—if anything happens to me, they will know that you are responsible. First they have instructions how to torture Ida here before they rape and then kill her.

"Next they will find your two children, Billy and Pauline, and they will torture them before they kill them. You, they will force you to live. You'll spend the rest of your life realizing that you caused your whole family to be tortured unbearably, and then killed.

"Think about that for a long time, Ray, before you even think about harming me or any of mine."

Renshew tipped his hat at Ida, then waved at Ray and walked down the stairs and out of the house. When Ida heard him leave the back door, she rushed to Ray, kissed him and cut off his bindings with a pair of scissors.

She treated his forehead cut, then her own. They fell into each other's arms and cried, then sat on the bed as he looked at her cut forehead again. The slices were not as deep as he had feared.

Slowly he shook his head.

"Ida, I don't know what to say. The man is a monster. He's thought of everything. I had planned on killing all three of them, but now, I can't. I can't risk the chance of his hurting you."

They hugged each other, and Ray cried again. "It's all because of that damn letter I wrote."

Ida wiped away his tears. She worked up a smile.

"So what's hurt? I'm the same as ever. I'm a little tired right now and I'll be sore for a few days, but nothing is damaged, nothing is worn out, and I can't get pregnant anymore. Remember the Eskimos loan out their wives to their friends. Frenchmen hire out their wives to tourists. What's to hurt?

"One of these days somebody is going to get Tom Renshew by his balls and chop them off. I want to be there to listen to him scream!"

Ray Krause looked at his wife in amazement. She was a solid rock. She had just been raped fifteen times, and she was the one trying to make *him* feel better.

"Let's go downstairs. I need to get the fire going and put on some water. I'm sure you'll want a good long hot bath. Then I have to open the store again. I want to watch for that man I talked to before. I just might have some more information for him about Tom Renshew."

Ida Krause smiled. "That's my man! Renshew just thinks he broke our spirit. We haven't even started to fight yet!"

Ray kissed his wife and hurried down the steps to get the fire going in the kitchen range. He wanted to be in the store the rest of the afternoon hoping he could spot the man from the government.

When Tom Renshew rode back down Main Street after the two hour session with Ida, he felt like a drink. He sent his two men in the Silver Dollar Saloon, said he would meet them later, and stopped in front of Frances's sewing shop. He eased the door open, heard the bell tinkle and waited for her to come out of the back room.

The girl who came out was not Frances. He frowned.

"Is Frances here?"

"Not right now. I work for her, can I help you?"

Renshew felt he knew the girl, but he couldn't be

sure. She had dark hair cut short and piled on top of her head. It showed off her long neck and high-lighted her brown eyes. One dimple dented a cheek.

It couldn't be! It was, the little whore from the Last Dollar Saloon!

"Virgin, isn't it? A strange name for a whore. You're the one who got my boy killed."

"And you're Tom Renshew who should have been the one killed. Get out."

"Don't order me around, whore."

"I'm not a whore. I work for Frances." She lifted a .32 caliber six-gun from under the counter and cocked the hammer. "You get out or I'll kill you. Plain enough?"

Renshew laughed.

Virgin closed her eyes and pulled the trigger.

The .32 caliber slug slammed out the four inch barrel, tore into Tom Renshew's left arm six inches below his elbow and broke the bone. He screamed in pain, grabbed his wrist and rushed out the door heading for the doctor's officer. He was half way there before he remembered the old doctor had died.

Frances was the one who patched up broken bones. Slowly he walked back to the sewing shop and looked inside. Frances was there and motioned him in. She had towels and hot water ready, also a bucket of water and a can of plaster of paris and twenty two-inch strips of sheets ready to wrap a cast around a broken arm.

Frances stared at him a moment. "Don't matter who gets hurt, I dig out bullets or set broken arms. Come right in and set down and have a long shot of whiskey. From the looks of that arm, you're going to do better half drunk."

13

Spur got back to his room in the hotel after dark on the same day he talked with Chief Many Winters. He was not convinced that the chief knew nothing about the raids that must have been carried out under the guise of hunting parties.

The young bucks must have a cache of the stolen goods somewhere along with the rifles. The old chief would have a tough time getting the long guns away from the renegade bucks. Spur would have to work at it from this end as well.

By now he was totally convinced that Tom Renshew was the main cause of the trouble. Renshew maintained his control over vast amounts of Dakota Territory that he didn't own. His actual land owning was probably minimal. Spur had seen it happen with other greedy ranchers.

They owned some land, controlled the rest by their presence, bluff, posting, and running off legitimate setters, homesteaders and those legally buying land.

In this case the contracted Indian raids and the

murders of the new settlers kept the land free of squatters for Renshew. At the same time the raids put the fear of death into any settler who looked at promising land that was available for home-steading. So far it had worked fine. That was about to come to an end.

Spur left his horse at the livery, told them to feed and rub it down and keep it available for him. He might need it soon.

Walking back to his hotel, he knew he had several options. He could call out Tom Renshew and hope to kill him in a shootout. He could try to find the supply of guns used to pay off the Indians. He could wait for Chief Many Winters to stop the Indian raiders from his camp.

Of the three options the second seemed most pro-ductive. If he could find the supply of rifles and destroy them, it would effectively cut off any more immediate Indian raids. It was worth a try.

The white girl he had seen haunted him. There must be someone he could ask about missing or kidnapped white girls. From the way she ran with the Indian girls she had been with them for a long time, perhaps years. That would make it harder. She was eight or nine. He would ask somebody. There was no immediate worry about her. First the rifles, then the girl.

The desk clerk gave Spur two messages when he picked up his key. In his room, Spur lit a lamp, then read the notes. Both were sealed in envelopes.

The one from Virgin was short. "Spur. I've moved in with Frances. She's a wonderful person, the mother I almost never had. I feel safe and needed for the first time . . . ever! Oh, Tom Renshew was in the shop today. I shot him. Frances fixed up his broken left arm. He hates me for sure now.

"Don't worry, I never go on the street now without my .32 pistol. I even practiced so I can shoot without closing my eyes. Don't worry. Come see me. Miss you. Virgin."

She shot Renshew? He chuckled. He wished he could have been there to see that.

The second note was from Ray Krause. "Harding, or whoever you are. Vital that I see you as soon as possible. May have more important information about Renshew. He and two of his men raped my wife today. They made me watch. I want to charge him with crimes. How can I do it with this sheriff?"

"See me as soon as you can."

"He told me he was teaching me a lesson not to tell lies about him. He told my wife she had to submit or he would kill me. It was brutal. I demand some satisfaction! . . . Ray."

Spur sprawled on the bed, hands behind his head staring at the ceiling. Renshew was pushing. He was scared. It all could help. Bat Masterson's humiliation of him, his son's death, and now his attack on Ray and his wife.

Spur wished Bat Masterson had stayed around town a little longer. As soon as he had made sure his suspect was not in town, he rode back to Colorado.

The Secret Service agent wished that he could rush out to the Renshew place and search it tonight. But he was in no shape for a tough assignment like that. He was bone weary and dirty from the long ride.

Spur ordered up a tub of hot water and took a long, steaming bath. No one bothered him. He fell into bed about ten that evening and never stirred until after nine o'clock the next morning. He checked his watch, turned over and slept until noon.

When he got up he was fully rested; he had a meal

in the dining room, then went to see Ray Krause at the store.

Quickly Ray told Spur about the death threat to Ray's family if anything happened to Renshew.

"It's a bluff, Ray. Those are tough kinds of arrangements to make, and once the man with the money is dead, few of the threats ever get carried out."

Ray shook his head. "I don't care. I won't take the chance. I'm sending Ida and the kids to her sister's place down in Bismarck. I'm sending a letter with her to give to the police.

"After they're out of town, I want to charge Renshew and his two men with rape, kidnapping, and assault with a deadly weapon. Is there any way we can do that the way the law is controlled in this town?"

Spur thought a moment. Then he nodded. "After we get Renshew on the run, I'll get myself appointed as a special county prosecutor, arrest the sheriff, and get the law back to working. First we have to shake up Renshew."

Spur told him how he planned to do it.

"Hope to God it works. If it don't, I'm closing up the store soon as my family is safe. Then I'm taking my best hunting rifle and two hundred rounds, and I'm going hunting for Tom Renshew!"

"Good way to get yourself killed, Ray. Leave Renshew up to me. He's my problem. I promise to keep him for a trial, an honest one. Now, I need some supplies. Ten sticks of dynamite, five blasting caps and twenty feet of fuse."

Ray nodded. "Now it sounds like we're getting somewhere. I hope you blow his house into kindling!"

Spur took his wrapped purchase back to his hotel

and hid it under his bed. He went to the duly elected District Attorney, and found him ensnared in his own private law practice, and with practically no county business.

"Not a lot of people here, fairly law abiding. Not many cases to prosecute for the people. We had a shooting last year and held a trial. Turned out it was a call out, a fair fight, so we dismissed it."

The man was curious. "You have some special reason to see me? Some crime you think the county should prosecute?"

"Yes, several, but I'm not sure you're the man I want to handle the work."

"Sir! I'm the District Attorney. Any prosecution must begin right here in my office."

Spur snorted. "Maybe that's why there hasn't been much legal work done in this county for the past four or five years." Spur turned and walked out leaving the man fuming.

He had tried to upset the prosecutor to see what he would do. The answer seemed that he would not do much. Spur stopped by and saw Virgin for a time, complimented her on her new hairdo and then went for an early steak dinner at the hotel. He then cleaned his guns, and checked out the horse he had used. It would be ready.

Spur rode away from town just before dark. He headed south, but as soon as he was out of sight of the town, he turned and moved back north toward the home spread of the Diamond D. He was going to pay a non-social call on Mr. Renshew and hands, and if he was lucky, they wouldn't even know he was there—until he had left.

By the time he arrived a half mile from the ranch buildings, it was solidly dark. The quarter moon that had been growing night by night was covered with high clouds that were not moving.

Spur tied his horse in some willow and cotton-woods near the river and took his package of dynamite and worked slowly toward the buildings.

They would have some kind of guards out, Spur was sure. Most big ranches could afford the luxury of night watchmen. He was half way there when he saw the first one. A man with a rifle over his shoulder left the outhouse and strolled to the far edge of the barn. There he vanished into the shadows.

This guard at least knew what he was supposed to be doing. Spur lay in the grass for fifteen minutes. The man never left the shadows. He could be inside the barn, might have moved to the far side of the barn, or just be waiting there impossible to see.

Spur had studied the Apache. He had seen a brave move across a desert landscape so slowly that he was almost impossible to see. He blended with the sand, and moved slowly one limb at a time so there would be no sudden action to catch the eye.

Unless you were watching one specific area where the Indian was, he could move twenty yards right in front of you thirty or forty yards away and you'd never see him.

Now Spur drew on some of his Indian skills and moved toward the barn slowly. He crawled through the plains grass, then at the edge of the barnyard, he slipped behind the corral fence and blended with a post.

He had all night. For five minutes Spur stood there without moving. He heard a door close in the barn, then a shadow merged at the side of the barn, paused, then walked through the open area to the well house forty yards away and slightly uphill.

Spur felt it was fitting that the well should be

some distance from the barn and the manure. He reached back and came up with a small fact: water will leach itself pure after it passes through six feet of light gravel.

As the guard left, Spur slid around the corral and stepped through a partly open back door in the big barn. It was typical frontier construction. Built to house horses, maybe a milk cow or two and lots of room for hay and harness. A buggy and a wagon also were housed there.

He began a quick search. The guard would be back sometime. Spur had to be ready for him.

Spur probed in feed bins, checked under sacks of grain, kicked through a thin pile of hay and leaned against the wall a moment listening.

A door squeaked. Spur squatted behind six bales of hay and waited. The guard came in, carrying a lantern. He swung it around, shining the light in corners and through the stalls. Spur's hand closed around a three gallon milk bucket. He pitched it so it landed behind the guard.

"What the hell?" The cowboy with the light spun around and Spur's old .44 slammed down on his head, jolting him to the barn floor. Spur grabbed the upset lantern before it could do any damage. He turned the flame down.

He tied the guard's feet with his own belt, then tied his hands behind him with his kerchief. Spur took his own kerchief and used it as a simple gag through his mouth, but nothing that would strangle the man.

Spur knew he had to work faster now. He kicked into a second pile of hay but could tell nothing. He found a three-tined pitchfork and stabbed it into the hay. Half way around he hit something hard.

Two minutes later he had forked enough hay away

so he could see the army rifle boxes. They were in the original shipping boxes made of wood, and Spur knew each should hold six rifles. He opened the hasp and lifted the lid on the first box.

Inside were six brand-new, army-ready Spencer repeating rifles. The kind of weapons the young bucks would kill for. Had killed for.

The Secret Service agent counted the boxes. Twenty of them. All full, which meant a hundred and twenty rifles. Enough to start a full-scale Indian rebellion!

Spur worked quickly now, tore open the boxes and dumped the rifles in a pile on the floor. He began to sweat when he was half through. A far off voice called from somewhere. Spur froze. Nothing else happened. He heard a screen door slam and then it was quiet.

Doggedly he dumped box after box until he had an expensive stack of weapons on top of the hay. He dug into them and planted the dynamite. Fixed it so the sticks would detonate each other. He put two caps into the pile of dynamite and rifles. He examined his fuse. It was twenty feet long. He set the fuse into one dynamite cap and inserted the explosive detonator into a hole he had pushed into the dynamite.

The fuse would lead almost to the back door and should take twenty minutes to detonate. The explosion would set the hay on fire as well. What rifles the dynamite didn't destroy, the fire should.

Spur dumped the rest of the dynamite caps on the sticks of powder, then dragged the unconscious guard to the back door. He ran back in, checked everything again in the darkness, then went back to the fuse. He lit it with a sulphur match, watched to be sure it began sputtering.

The fuse was supposed to burn a foot a minute, but you could never be sure from one fuse to the next. He carried the guard thirty yards away through the corral, dumped him by the posts and looked over the ranch yard carefully.

He saw nobody. Quietly he jogged away from the barn and toward his house.

He was barely five minutes away, but almost to his horse, when the explosion tore through the stark and darkly quiet Dakota night.

He turned in time to see the outline of the barn glow with the heat and fire of the blast before the roof split and fell inward. Streamers of fire blasted into the sky. He could imagine parts of rifles falling around the barnyard.

Then the clapping roar of the explosion reached across the land and slapped him, making his head buzz for a moment.

Gusts of wind whipped at him from the concussion, then it was gone and he saw the glow of the fire rise and grow. Soon it was a roaring inferno.

He heard cries from the bunkhouse and the main ranch house. Now and then he could see a man running in the light. Then he saw six horsemen streak through the flare of the fire.

He lifted on his horse and rode south at a canter. The horsemen would be flailing around in the darkness, shooting at anything that moved.

Before he had ridden half a mile he could hear rifle bullets going off in the fire. They sounded like firecrackers. The fire and the explosion would cut short Renshew's supply of rifles to control the Indians. The only trouble was, Spur still had to prove that Renshew was doing the gun running.

The fire billowed higher. The whole barn would burn to the ground. Nothing the crew could do would save it. With the rifle rounds going off, nobody was going to mount a bucket brigade.

Spur continued his ride back to town. He put the horse in the livery, paid the hostler, and carried his Spencer over his shoulder as he walked back to his hotel.

He went in the side door of the Far Northern Hotel and directly to his room. His key unlocked the door and he pushed it open. Before he could take a quick breath he drew the six-gun from his holster.

Someone was in his room.

Faint light from the hall penetrated the small room and before Spur could move to light a lamp, a girlish laugh giggled up from the covers.

"Don't shoot, Spur McCoy. I'll marry you."

"Virgin. You could have left a light on. A person could get shot that way."

"Sorry. I was tired and I had a nap while I waited for you."

He lit a lamp and closed the door and locked it. She stood on the bed and motioned to him. He walked over in front of her and their noses were the same height.

Gently she kissed him on the cheek, then on his lips.

"I've missed you, and I want you, and can I keep my feet warm against your back tonight?"

"If I didn't know better, I'd guess that you weren't a virgin."

She pouted. "Sir! You know very well that I'm a virgin." She looked at him closely. "You've been on a long ride or something. Let me give you a sponge bath and then relieve any serious swelling that I find on your body. Then I have some strange news for you."

She washed him in the cold water of the basin,

working down his chest and arms, then stripping off his boots, and pants until he was naked.

"See, you do have a swelling," she said with a giggle. "I know how to reduce that."

Nearly an hour later they lay in the bed coming down from a furious pair of climaxes. She drifted off to sleep and he kissed her awake.

"You are as sexy and as marvelous as ever. Now, tell me your rather disturbing news."

"Oh, that. I'll get a lawyer, let him handle it. I can't really believe he's serious."

"What's serious?"

"I had a visit from the District Attorney today. A citizen has charged me with assault with intent to kill. I'm to have a first hearing in a week and am supposed to have an attorney."

"Intent to kill? What in the . . . Who could . . . Oh, no, it's Tom Renshew, isn't it? He's mad because you shot his arm."

"I could just as well have killed him. I closed my eyes."

"Figures. He'll get you charged and a trial date set and then he'll settle out of court, say he'll drop the charges if you leave town and never come back."

"I won't go. This is my home now, and I have a job here."

"That, too, he doesn't like. I'll work on it tomorrow. Right now I want to get some sleep."

Spur laughed softly. "Mr. Renshew may have a more important problem to worry about right now at his ranch. That's where I've been. I blew up 120 Spencer repeating rifles and burned down his big barn. He won't have anything to pay off the Indians with now for raiding."

"That's great! Anything to hurt that big bastard! Does he know it was you? Will he come after you with shotguns?"

"I don't know. He'll be as mad as bat piss, I know that. But he won't have a lead—except maybe Ray Krause."

Spur kicked out of bed and began pulling on his clothes.

"What are you doing?"

"I've got to warn Ray Krause to hide out some-where. Renshew is liable to come at him with ten guns and kill his whole family. I've got to get there first!"

14

Tom Renshew stood in the big ranch yard and watched his barn burn to the ground. One of his men had come up with half of a new Spencer rifle. It had been blasted into pieces. At once Renshew knew someone had found the rifles and destroyed them, and burned down his barn and six tons of hay in the process.

His first question was who. At first he suspected Ray Krause. He would have the dynamite. But Krause was too scared, too much of a towner ever to do something like this. He remembered the mystery man who came in on the stage and killed his son and vanished. It could be him. But where was he?

Renshew saw the last of the barn walls crash down, one outward, the other into the fire. Any rifles not blasted apart would be melted into one big puddle of metal by the time the fire was burned out.

He didn't know the who, but he would find out. Just where did this leave him? He could try one more payoff to Dog Piss and his men with older, used rifles. Six rifles for one raid on one small rancher just at the edge of his land. That would be a good capper to the Indian scare, and get that last bothersome squatter away from his land.

Yes! One more and then he would be through with the Indians. They were too damn unpredictable anyway. He sent word for Wolf Vincent to come. Tom was still not used to the damn cast on his left arm, and his arm hurt like hell. He was forever hitting it on things. It was a nuisance. In six weeks it would come off and he'd find out how badly he was going to hurt Virgin. She would catch all sorts of hell.

Wolf Vincent was a half breed, half Yanktonai, and he knew their ways. He had left the tribe years ago, became a town Indian and at last signed on with Renshew to help him get along with the Yanktonai. Now he was the contact with Dog Piss. Renshew walked off into the darkness with the Breed and explained it carefully.

"Tell Dog Piss one more raid. One ranch for six rifles. It has to be tomorrow night. We'll meet at a new place and someone will lead him to the target. Got that?"

Wolf nodded.

"Take a hundred rounds of ammo for the rifles. Tell Dog Piss that's a little present for him. And keep all this from old Chief Many Winters."

Tom slid a twenty dollar gold piece from his pocket and handed it to the Breed. "You still corn-holing that little squaw up there? The one with the slit nose?"

Wolf took the coin, touched it to his forehead in salute and slid into the darkness. Someday the big mouth boss white chief was going to step too far over the line. Wolf had quick thoughts of how he would kill Tom Renshew, then he shrugged, picked up the rifle rounds, and saddled his horse from the second corral. He had a twenty-five mile ride and he had to get there before daylight.

The night of the barn fire at the Diamond D, Spur McCoy had realized he may have put Ray Krause in danger. He had hurried over to the Krause home and banged on the door. An upstairs window opened and a cautious voice called out, but nobody answered at the window.

"What the hell you want?"

"Ray, it's me, Harding. We need to talk."

Krause's head edged up in the darkened window. "Yeah, Okay. I'll be right down."

They talked at the back door. Spur told him about the rifles.

"You were right, it was Renshew supplying the Indians. But after I blew them up, I realized he might come after you. Can you move somewhere, stay with somebody?"

"Family is gone. Sent them on the afternoon stage. I'll just load up my shotguns, I got four of them, and my two rifles and three hand guns, and wait for the bastard. I'm through running."

"I doubt he'll be here tonight. Want me to stay?"

"No, I'll be fine. If he gets me, I'll take more than one of them with me. It had to come to this sooner or later."

They talked a few minutes more, then Spur returned to his hotel and his bed and became a footwarmer.

The next day Spur talked to the one lawyer in town. He was an honest man named Hal Zenger. He had heard about the shooting, and about the charges.

"Be happy to defend Virginia. We can come up with all sorts of nasty testimony about Renshew. Problem is if the judge will let us use it. The regular circuit judge is one of Renshew's oldest buddies. You know that Renshew owns the District Attorney and the sheriff?''

"I know it. Maybe we can get a special judge?"

"Been tried, never worked."

Spur scowled. "Do what you can. Get the hearing postponed so you can secure additional information about your client's mental stability from her former residence in Illinois. You can make the judge believe that."

Spur left feeling somewhat better. He talked with Ray in the hardware store.

"I grew up in the retail business," Spur said. "All sorts, from haberdashery to pots and pans."

"How am I doing here?" Ray asked.

"Not bad at all. If we both can live through the next week."

Ray turned grim. "We have a small protest group I don't think you know about. Not exactly vigilantes, more on the defensive side. We were all set to get something done before the massacre. Three of our men were among those killed."

"I'm sorry."

"Not as sorry as they were. That cuts down our ranks, but we've still got a few homesteaders. If they get in trouble, they're supposed to have one person to cut and run and come and get us. Hasn't worked yet, but never can tell."

Spur took Ray to dinner at noon. He simply closed the doors until he came back. It happened all the time. Spur was trying to be a casual bodyguard to the merchant, but he knew it wouldn't work for long.

By two o'clock back at the store, Ray threw him out.

"I don't need a bleeding bodyguard. Now get out of here."

Spur had told him who he was, his real name and everything.

"I'll go, just don't get violent," Spur yelped. "Tomorrow is when I start my campaign to bring Renshew to justice. I don't know if it will work or not, but I'm going to give it one hell of a try."

"How?"

"Use the Bat Masterson approach. Start telling the absolute truth about Tom. Scream his sins from the rooftops and challenge the district attorney not to indict him. If I'm lucky I can work up enough public support for my charges that the D.A. will be forced to obey the law, and the sheriff will have to cooperate or resign. It just might work."

"Sure, and the wind might blow sweet perfume out of the nearest outhouse hole, but I doubt it."

Spur went to Frances's shop and told her about the small white girl in the Indian camp.

"Happens quite often out here, Mr. McCoy. I haven't heard of any family claiming to have lost a girl. Which means it could be the rest of her family is all dead. That's common practice among the plains Indians. They kill the family, save the girls for brides or slaves and take off. There's no one to come rescue them."

"Do any of them ever come back, after a time, say a year or more?"

"Older women, maybe, if rescued. Once a woman in her twenties was taken and rescued six months later. By that time she was completely crazy."

Virgin spoke up. "With the kids it would be easier. The only problem is, I've heard once a white child is with a tribe for a year or more, they *become Indian.* Most likely the child would not want to come back."

Frances adjusted a dress she was fitting on a dummy figure. She took pins from her mouth.

"Did you hear about Cynthia Ann Parker? She

was kidnapped in 1836 by the Comanches when she was nine. She grew up as a Comanche, married one of the tribe's chiefs. She could ride better than the other squaws, hunt better than most of the braves, and bore the chief several children. She's still alive as far as I know, still a Comanche."

Spur had heard what he needed to know. There was no immediate need to charge back up to the Yanktonai and demand to see the white girl. He could concentrate on putting together a public and private assault on the crooked courts and lawmen of the county.

Three horses with Diamond D brands worked closer to the new meeting point with the Indians. It was only slightly after six o'clock in the evening. It would not be dark for two hours yet. The meeting had been arranged by Wolf Vincent, the Breed who sat on the edge of the Souris River with Dog Piss throwing rocks into the water.

Tom Renshew and his son, Harry, rode through the cooling air. Behind them came a pack horse with the six rifles tied to it. They arrived at the meeting place promptly at the six-thirty time.

Dog Piss swept out of the brush on his war pony brandishing a six foot long lance tipped with steel.

"Who is this man?" He shouted pointing the lance at Harry.

Wolf rode up and told him, then Wolf rode and sat on his horse behind the Renshews.

"Why another raid so quick?" Dog Piss asked, his voice a whine.

"Because it could be the last one," Renshew said. "I offer you six rifles, not new ones, but good, practical weapons."

Dog Piss slid from his horse. One of his men darted in on foot and touched the war pony's bridal and it remained still. The Yanktonai went to the pack horse, cut the twine binding up the leather coverings and caught the rifles.

One by one he looked at them and dropped them to the ground.

"Not good weapons!" he flared. "You trick Dog Piss!"

The Indian jumped up, his face filled with anger. He made a hand signal and four braves came out of the brush each with one of the Spencer repeating rifles aimed at the three men still on their horses.

"You have tricked Dog Piss. You make him angry. No more can Dog Piss trust roundeye!"

"You're been paid well for your work. One more job, and the six rifles are good weapons." Renshew might as well have been talking to a tornado.

Dog Piss rushed forward, jerked Harry off his horse and pulled him down.

"Don't touch my son!" Renshew boomed. A rifle round slammed a foot over his head.

"Not move!" Dog Piss screeched. He stripped off the young man's shirt, threw his revolver into the brush, then using his knife drew a straight blood line across Harry's chest.

Harry screamed and fell into the dirt.

"Dog Piss never trust white chief again!" he thundered. He caught Harry's horse, leaped on board. Two of his men swept in and each picked up three of the rifles and vanished into the brush leading Dog Piss's war pony.

A moment later the band of six Yanktonai braves charged away through the trees and up the river to the north.

Renshew slid from his mount and hurried to his son still trembling in the grass. The cut was not deep. It would heal with no scar.

Renshew lifted his pistol but the Indians were far out of range.

"I'll kill that bastard if I ever see him again!" Renshew bellowed.

Wolf Vincent rode up on his horse, dismounted and helped Harry into his saddle. Wolf took a few steps away from the horse and leaped on the nag's back behind Harry.

"Mr. Renshew, it's nothing personal. Chief Many Winters found out about Dog Piss's raids down here and he was mad as a tree full of hornets. He told Dog Piss no more raids or he would be banned from the tribe. This act Dog Piss put on was just to save his dignity . . . and to get the horse and the rifles."

Renshew swore and stumbled as he went back to his mount. He got on board despite his broken left arm.

For two miles, Tom Renshew didn't say a word. Then he turned to Harry. "The damn Indians won't do it, so we'll fix it so it looks like Indians did it. Harry, you and Wolf take five or six men and ride over to the Unger ranch tonight. Burn them out, run them off the place. You don't have to kill them, just scare them off and burn down everything. Make them think you're Indians. Wolf will know how to do it."

"But Dad, don't you think we should let this settle down a while first?"

"Damnit, no! I told you what to do. As soon as we get back to the ranch, you get over there. It's only four miles from town and it's damn near on our property line. I want them off that piece of land!"

Spur had just finished cleaning his six-gun in his hotel room when someone pounded on the door.

"McCoy! You in there?"

Spur jumped to the door, his six-gun freshly
loaded. He pulled open the panel from the side and
saw Ray Krause.

"Bring your rifle and six-gun and plenty of
rounds. Looks like the Indians are hitting another
settler. A little ranch just outside of town."

Spur grabbed his Spencer, his hat, two boxes of
rounds and ran down the hallway and steps to the
street. Ray had a horse for him. He found out the
details as they rode. Two other men were supposed
to be getting ready to go help the rancher.

"That little group we set up has a warning
system. When the Unger's place got hit about an
hour ago, the oldest boy sneaked out of the house in
the dark, got a horse and hightailed it to town. Kid
said they were ready for them."

"They better be damn good and ready if it's the
Yanktonai. I saw what they did to that other place."

They rode hard for a mile, walked their horses,
then rode hard again. The place was only four miles
away. They could hear shooting when they were a
mile off.

"Boy said they put a slate roof on the ranch house
so it couldn't be burned easy. They put up logs
around the walls like a fort, leaned them up against
the house."

"Hope like hell we're not too late."

"It's a good sign that they're still shooting."

From a quarter of a mile away they saw a fire
start. It erupted and burned fiercely.

"Got to be a barn to burn that fast," Ray said.

Three hundred yards from the house Spur
stopped. They watched for rifle fire. Soon it became
clear that those in the house were alive and fighting.

In a rough line about fifty yards from the house
Spur could see five or six firing positions. It was too
dark to pick out the men, but he saw the muzzle

flashes and drifts of blue smoke from the powder.

The moon, working toward half full, slid from behind clouds and Spur grinned. He took his Spencer, moved up twenty yards closer and waited for the next man to fire from below.

He saw the flash, and put three quick rounds into the area. Someone screamed in pain. He lifted his sights and did the same pattern on the next man who fired in the line. This time there was no reaction. Twice more he found ambushers shooting at the house. Twice more he fired a pattern around the man.

Ray found a position and began to do the same thing working his own two targets from the other end of the rough line. For two minutes there was no more firing. Another minute went by, then another. From somewhere farther back from the house, they heard hoofbeats, as three or four horses pounded away into the prairie heading north.

Spur bellowed at the house.

"Unger family in the house! We're friends. You all right?"

"Mostly. They gone?"

"Think so. Stay put."

Spur and Krause worked slowly toward the firing position. They found the first spot, but no one was there. On down they found a small pile of brass casings beside a white man. He had taken a rifle slug in the head.

"That one looks like one strange Indian," Krause said.

Twenty feet farther along a man screamed at them.

"You come any closer I'll blow you to hell!"

"Not likely," Spur shouted back. "You're wounded or you'd be running like the rest. Throw out your rifle and we'll get you some medical help."

There was a pause.

"Hell, why not?" A rifle sailed over some low brush.

The man stood, his hands in the air. "Come on, damnit, I'm half way bleeding to death."

Spur ran up, made sure he had no knife or hideout gun, then looked at his leg. Spur tore up the man's shirt to fashion a makeshift bandage and stopped the blood. Then they went up to the house.

Krause had hurried to the house and told them it was all clear. When the Ungers brought out a lantern, Krause stared at the captured man and snorted.

"Hi, Quinn. Old man Renshew gonna be mad as hell when he finds out your Indian raid went sour. We've got the son-of-a-bitch dead to rights now. Bet the dead man out there is from his ranch, too. I think we just got the evidence we needed to ramrod that yellow bellied bastard into a hangman's noose!"

Spur agreed. Larry Unger thanked the two men, and said he'd be glad to ride into town and swear out a warrant against Quinn, and make sure he got locked up.

"Fine idea," Spur said. "I just got me a hankering to take over the county jail. I have a piece of paper in my bag that will shake up Sheriff Sweet till hell freezes over. Why don't we all take a ride into town."

Krause took a lantern and a horse and went out and brought back the dead body.

"We'll take this one in too," Ray said. "Not sure what his name is, but he worked for Renshew out at the ranch. Christ but it's going to be an interesting evening when we move in on that county jail!"

15

The small party came into town quietly. It was about ten o'clock by that time, and most of the respectable citizens were sleeping. One deputy slept in the usually empty jail. Spur rousted him by banging on the locked jail house door.

"Yeah, yeah, coming. What the hell!"

When the door opened Spur kicked it forward bouncing the sleepy deputy backward.

"Are you a sworn deputy sheriff?" Spur demanded.

"Hell yes, who are you?"

"My name is Spur McCoy. I'm a Federal law officer with the U.S. Secret Service. I'm requisitioning your facility for the next few weeks. I'm requesting that you go find the sheriff and bring him here, at once."

"Can't do that. I don't know you."

"Fine." Spur drew the .44 so quickly the deputy gawked. "Move to the rear, please, you'll sleep in one of the cells for the rest of the night. Move!"

Five minutes later they had the dead man identified as a hand at the Diamond D ranch. He was turned over to the undertaker. Spur sent for the lawyer he had talked to before. By the time Zenger got there things were well in hand.

"Mr. Zenger. Come in, glad to see you again. I'm Spur McCoy, we met earlier. You and I have some business. I represent the U.S. Government and I want to retain you to draw up charges against several people. They must be ready by ten o'clock tomorrow morning. Can you do that?"

Zenger looked at the prisoner, was told about the dead man and who was behind the fake Indian raid.

"My pleasure. All we have to do is suspend the District Attorney some way, or convince him to do his sworn duty. By morning I'll have an idea on that. The sheriff will be no problem. If we have enough indictments and enough fire power by then he'll swing our way. He's a coward and a real asshole, but he's not stupid."

Spur found the coffee pot, fired up the little stove and soon had a full two quarts of coffee boiling. It was going to be a long working night.

Zenger began by interviewing Frank Unger, the rancher who had been attacked by the fake Indians. Within half an hour he had the facts and drew up the indictment of the dead man, Quinn—the wounded hand caught at the ranch, and Thomas Renshew who hired them. Since a death took place, the two live men were charged with murder.

Next Zenger talked to Ray Krause and got information from him to charge Renshew, and his hands, Wyoming and Jed, with kidnapping, assault with a weapon with intent to kill, and multiple counts of rape and sodomy.

Spur talked with Zenger and gave him the facts to

file federal charges against Renshew of selling repeating rifles to the Yanktonai Indians.

"Also I want you to find the names of those twenty settlers who were killed by the Indians. I want twenty murder indictments against Renshew for those deaths as well, naming him as the man who hired the Indians to do the killing, and making him equally guilty. Will that keep you busy until morning?"

Zenger grinned. "At least. I'll have my wife come help me write up the paper. This is something I've dreamed of getting to do for the two years I've lived here and watched Renshew run this county. He's through now, that's for damn sure!"

Spur sent back to the jail cells and woke up Quinn. The man came awake with a groan, moved his leg and swore.

"So you're awake, Quinn. How would you like to spend the next ten years in a Federal prison for attempted murder?"

Quinn stared at him. "Mr. Renshew will have me out of here by daylight."

"Not a chance, Quinn. I've taken ove the jail, thrown the deputy into a cell, and if the sheriff won't cooperate with us, I'll jail him and charge him with complicity in a dozen felonies. The District Attorney can cooperate or resign, I'll see to that with the first daylight.

"What I want to talk to you about is saving your ass. You know what immunity is?"

Quinn shook his head.

"That means we have you dead to rights on serious charges. But if you cooperate with us, and testify for the state, we'll agree not to prosecute you, and after Renshew's trail, you'll be a free man. Sound interesting?"

"Yeah. Yeah. I want it in writing, all legal. You got a lawyer out there?"

Twenty minutes later, Zenger had drawn up a paper to give Quinn immunity for his full cooperation.

Ray Krause came in with a pad of paper and two sharpened pencils.

"Now, Mr. Quinn, we need some facts. Who contacted the Yanktonai for Renshew?"

"A breed named Wolf Vincent. He's half Yanktonai. Speaks both English and the Indian lingo."

"Fine. Did you ever go on the exchange when Renshew gave the Indians the rifles?"

"Once."

"Tell us about it. Was Renshew along?"

They listened as Quinn outlined the trip, the exchange, the orders.

Spur watched Krause writing it down.

"Good, Quinn, you're earning your freedom. You'll be testifying to most of this in court, you understand that?"

The man nodded.

"Fine. Now, about tonight. Tell us about the orders to burn out the Ungers. Who gave them, who went on the raid, how it was supposed to look like an Indian operation."

It was nearly morning when Quinn stopped talking. Ray Krause had a tired hand, and a dozen pages of notes. Spur grinned. He had a case that any jury in the land would use to convict Renshew, even if he was the biggest man in the county.

When it was seven A.M., Spur let the deputy go, instruction him to tell the sheriff and the District Attorney they were needed at once at the jail. He scurried off, evidently glad that he was not caught up in the snowfall of indictments he heard them talking about.

The District Attorney arrived first, unshaven, sleepy eyed but angry and on edge.

He remembered Spur. Spur showed him his authorization and told him what he had done so far.

"Mr. Zenger will have twenty-four indictments of Thomas Renshew ranging from rape and sodomy to murder. Everyone in the county knows that Renshew owns the sheriff and you. He pays you twice what you get in salary from the county. We can prove it. Just what you do is up to you, but I'd advise you to switch sides, to file the indictments through your office, to send a delegation to arrest Renshew, and to request a special court be called in this district for a speedy trial. No bail should be allowed for Renshew."

The District Attorney sat down quickly in a chair in the sheriff's office. He stared at the list of felonies his benefactor was charged with. It sent his head reeling. How could this have happened? Then he looked at Spur's credentials again. United States Secret Service!

"Well, yes. This is the first time that I have been made privy to any wrongdoing by Mr. Renshew. It's a shock and a surprise, but I am a county law officer, and I will see that Mr. Renshew is brought to a speedy trial, just as any other citizen in this county would.

"My office will give complete cooperation with Mr. Zenger in preparing the indictments. In fact we could adjourn to my offices right now and expedite this matter."

Spur watched him. The man was not stupid. He had changed sides effortlessly.

"One more item. Sheriff Sweet does not know of

this yet. He's on his way here now. If for any reason he does not agree to cooperate in these matters, I'll be asking for an indictment of the sheriff as well and remove him from office. Do you agree?"

"Absolutely, Mr. McCoy. I'm sure Sheriff Sweet will go with us in this matter. Something this flagrant simply can't be ignored by the county law function."

They waited for the sheriff. He came a half hour later, and it was obvious the deputy had filled him in on the developments.

He bustled into his office, seemed surprised to see all the people there.

"I know about the crisis in the county. I know how Tom Renshew has been deceiving us all these years. Gentlemen, you have my complete and total cooperation, and all the power that my elective office of Sheriff can put behind it. I'll send a pair of deputies out to the Diamond D Ranch within the hour to bring in Renshew."

Spur wanted to relax, but it wasn't over yet. He did not expect the sheriff's deputies to have any luck finding Renshew. His spies in town would have reported what had happened this morning in the sheriff's office. He would realize he was wanted now and Spur didn't know what his reaction would be.

One thing he did know. He was hungry as a wounded she-bear and he needed a shave.

Back at his hotel room he eyed the bed with longing. Instead he shaved in cold water and was just washing off the shaving soap when someone knocked on his door.

He fisted iron and stepped silently to the side of the door.

"Who is it?" he asked.

"Little Red Riding Hood. Is the wolf at home?"

He opened the door and Virgin flew in. She grabbed him and kissed his lips and then spun away. She had on another new dress, pretty, and covering her chin, to wrist, to ankles.

"First, how do you like my new dress?" She charged on without waiting for an answer. "Next I changed my name, I'm really Virginia, so that's me from now on. Virginia McCoy. I don't want my old family name. And I just like the name McCoy. Any objections?"

She waited.

He shook his head and reached for his shirt which he buttoned, then opened his fly and stuffed the shirt into place and buttoned up.

She grinned. "At least I got to see close to the good stuff. Is it all true that I hear about Renshew? Him getting charged with murder and rape and . . . just everything?"

"True. We've got him hooked. Now we'll see if he can wiggle off the hook and get free."

"He'll never turn himself in. You've figured that out."

"True. Had breakfast?"

She shook her head. He caught up his hat, checked his .44 and took her down to the dining room. Spur ate enough for two ordinary men. Staying up did that to him, demanded more and more fuel for his body.

"Wow, I'm glad I won't have to feed you that much breakfast every morning like I would if we were married. We won't be, though, because I asked you and you never answered me, and anyway I know that you're the roaming, wandering type. With your job I guess you have to be, but all I can do is hope that you'll wander back this way once in a while."

Spur chuckled. "Wish I could get you to talk

sometime. You're too closed mouthed, Virginia."

They both laughed.

"So, now what?" she asked.

"We see what Renshew does, and we finish up the case. Then I take a ride up to the Yanktonai and see what I can find out about the little white girl."

"I figured that." She hesitated. "Don't . . ." she stopped. "Spur McCoy, I guess you know I love you, and I know you don't love me, but before you leave, could we have just one more night for me to remember? It's going to be a long, tough road for me here in Minot . . ."

"I promise. That won't be for a while. Depends on this case." Spur grinned at her, picked up her hand and kissed it. "Now don't you think you should be getting to work before you get fired?"

"Oh, my God! You're right!" She jumped up, touched his shoulder and hurried out the door.

Spur wondered how long it would take Renshew to react. If he knew what was going on, he might be in town right now. The chances were good that he would try to find Spur McCoy. By now he would tie the name to the name of the man on the stage who shot his son and started this whole scenario.

Spur decided to make it easy for him. It had been weeks since he'd sat in a chair outside a store, leaned back and relaxed. This seemed like a good time.

He picked Ray Krause's store and waved through the front window at the merchant who had his store open again. Spur took a chair and leaned back, then he sat down, took out his knife and did some work on his holster he figured might come in handy. Then he relaxed, let his hat come down part way over his eyes, but not enough to hide who he was.

He sat there for a half hour, then a shadow fell across his face and he looked at the cause. Three men stood ten feet away. The one in the middle was Tom Renshew. Spur moved his left hand cautiously, pushing back his hat. He left his right hand hanging near his holster.

"Well, the wanted man, Tom Renshew. I've heard of you. Killer of small children, buyer of massacres, gun runner to the Indians, rapist of innocent women. Quite a career."

"Don't move!" Renshew snarled. "You're covered." Spur saw that the man on the left had his six-gun drawn and aimed at him.

"Can't even fight your own fights, Renshew? Why not just gun me down in cold blood right now, or better let your hired killer do the dirty work for you. What is one more killing to a blooded bastard like you!"

Renshew's hand wavered over his holstered pistol.

"I don't need anyone to do my fighting for me. You're the one who gunned down my son, aren't you?"

"I found three men raping a woman on the boardwalk in the middle of the afternoon. They fired, I fired. They shot first. It's not my fault they missed. I didn't."

"Bastard! I've got you now. You'll hang proper! Wyoming, go get the sheriff!"

The man hesitated. "Tom, the sheriff ain't liking us much right now, remember?"

"Yeah, right. Put one round in his leg, slow him down some."

When Wyoming reached to draw his six-gun, Spur's right hand which still hung low next to his hog log, shifted only inches, the holster slanted upward a bit and the weapon fired. Wyoming went down with a .44 slug through his heart.

Before the other man could shoot, Spur's still

holstered gun barked again and Jed's right biceps splattered blood as a lead messenger crashed through muscle and into bone. He screamed, dropped his weapon and fell to the ground.

Spur sprang to his feet, his Colt drawn now and covering Renshew.

"Three on one are not polite odds, Mr. Renshew. Suppose we walk down and talk to the sheriff about it."

"No. Once I get inside that jail, I'll never come out. I've made enemies in town. I know that."

"Like Ray Krause? I'm surprised he hasn't put a pair of rifle slugs through your head by now. He's standing at the door with a Sharps."

Renshew looked that way. He sighed. "My son, Harry, said it couldn't last much longer. He said we'd have to pull back to the land we owned, or rent it from somebody. I can't operate that way."

"You won't have to worry about it, you'll be in prison."

Renshew shook his head. "Not a chance. You'll have to kill me. No prison."

Slowly he drew his pistol and held it muzzle down. "We've had some differences, McCoy. Understand you're a Government man, but you know the West. I can't go to prison. I'd die in a month. Might just as well do it now. Save the county the expense. On three I'm going to lift this .45 and shoot you. Be pleased to do that, make up for you killing Ed. Don't think I'll miss. I'm good with this. You either kill me, or I gun you down. No other way. You understand?"

"I do. You'll still go to prison."

"One."

"You could be out in fifteen years."

"Two."

"There's no need for this, Renshew!"

"Three."

Renshew lifted the .45. A fraction of a second before he fired, Spur's .44 blasted, the round slamming into Renshew's right shoulder, slamming him backward. Renshew fell into the dirt of the street, but held on to the weapon.

"Drop it, Renshew!"

The man in the dirt lifted the revolver again, Spur fired before Renshew could, the round tearing into Renshew's right wrist, smashing his arm away from the pistol. Spur walked forward to get the gun.

Renshew grabbed the iron with his left hand, pushed the muzzle against the side of his head. Spur blasted another round. This one hit the cylinder on Renshew's .45 and slammed it out of his hand before it fired.

Spur walked up and stared down at the dazed Renshew.

"Like I said, there was no need for this. You're going to hang or spend a long time in prison. Really doesn't matter to me."

As Spur finished, Frances, the tall, stately black woman, hurried up with a pan of hot water and a blanket of bandages and a bottle of alcohol.

Without a word she sat in the dirt beside Renshew. She stopped the flow of blood, then she cleaned and bandaged the two wounds. She crooned softly to him. Curiously it was a lullaby. Renshew looked at her and silent tears began to flow down his cheeks. Then he was crying openly. She cradled his head against her bosom and crooned the soft song, ignoring the suprised stares of the crowd of on-lookers.

They were still that way when the sheriff came a few minutes later and led Renshew to a jail cell.

Spur helped Frances stand, and walked with her up the street to her stitchery shop. Neither of them spoke. At the shop she touched his arm.

"It don't matter who hurt, I fix them up best I can. Mr. Renshew, he and me go way back. I helped birth him. Then his mamma die, and I stay on and care for him. His daddy good to me. I see him grow up, and I see him get rich and mean.

"But he's human, like the rest of us. He bleed, he get sad, he hate himself sometimes. Now, it's over." She looked up. "You understand?" Spur nodded.

"When he young man he father my only chile. Then later he kill my boy. Accident, he say. Now it all over." She reached for the door. Her usually bland black face took on the hint of a smile.

"Now, I have new chile. You no worry about Virginia. I take care of her. Nobody hurt the chile no more. Three years and I find her good husband. You see."

Frances reached out and kissed his cheek. "Spur man. You walk careful. You got to shoot, you shoot straight. You come back see us someday."

Without another glance she went in the door and closed it behind her.

16

Spur walked to the jail and went inside. The sheriff beamed at him.

"Mighty nice work, Mr. McCoy. Mighty nice. We have our man and a witness and I'll see that we get a good judge out here as soon as we can. You'll be around for the trial, of course."

Spur took off his hat and rubbed the headband, then slid the low crowned hat back in place.

"Hard to tell. You have all the evidence you need to convict him with Quinn and Ray and his wife. Wolf Vincent might turn state's evidence if you approached him just right. I'm not at all sure I'll still be hero unless that judge rushes."

"I sent a letter on the morning stage to the state capital in Bismarck. We should hear back in a few days."

Spur stood and planted his feet in front of the sheriff's desk. The small man peered up through his eye glasses.

"Sheriff, I'd be terribly disappointed in you if anything happened to Renshew. He's suicidal, so don't let him have anything he can hang himself with. No belt, no shoelaces, nothing. If he's going to hang, I want it after a trial, all legal and correct. I'll be gone for a few days. When I get back, I hope we have a trial date."

"We'll watch Renshew, you bet. He won't kill himself in my jail. He won't even get a razor. No sir!"

"Good." Spur turned and walked out of the jail and straight for Ray's store. Together they outfitted him for a ride, with food, trinkets to give away, six small hand mirrors, and more .56 caliber rounds for his Spencer.

Spur told him about the young white girl. Ray scowled for a minute.

"Can't remember hearing about any missing kids in this part of the country. Course she could have been traded from band to band half way across the West. Blond small girls are a real premium for some tribes." He hesitated. "You want some company? My family is still in Bismarck."

Spur considered it a moment. It would be a long, lonesome ride. At last he shook his head. "Thanks, but this is one I have to do alone. Chief Many Winters knows me, it will simply be easier to try to get the rifles back and ask about the small girl if there is no threat at all to his people."

It was noon when Spur left. He got the same horse from the stable he had used before. The ride was not difficult, the weather cooperated with only one brief shower near sundown. He moved at a leisurely pace and camped in a heavy thicket just off the river a short time before it got dark.

Spur had bacon and beans from a can for supper that night. He warmed his hands at the small fire, knowing he was fifteen miles from the outer limits of the Indians. He sliced bread from a loaf he bought at the bakery and made bean and bacon sandwiches to go with his coffee.

When the small fire burned down to coals, he banked them and stretched out on his blankets. He was not sure what he would find at the Yanktonai camp the next day.

Dog Piss would be an angry young buck, but probably the chief had straightened him out. It would be much easier if the chief had found the rifles and they were ready to haul back to Minot or to destroy. Spur had not decided what to do. First he had to get the rifles.

He listened to the night sounds as the wind died in the trees. Hawks, an owl, then a second. A coyote pined for a mate far off and an answering call came from closer by.

Later he thought he heard something like a wildcat, but he wasn't sure. He drifted off to sleep, content in the wide open, pleased that they had at least brought down a local tyrant, and happy that the locals had taken such a strong hand in doing it. There was hope for Dakota Territory yet.

In the morning he woke slowly, savoring the clean, fresh smell of the small woods, enjoying the sound of the Souris River as it gurgled over rocks in a small downslope. Then he had coffee, and pushed on upstream, following a deer trail along the bank, cutting across obvious loops in the water course, and making his first contact with the Yanktonai scouts about the same place he did last time.

This time he waved at them but had no evidence that they saw him. He was allowed to ride within a mile of the main camp before a pair of scouts rode out and met him.

He gave the sign of FRIEND, and the Indians

repeated it, then indicating he should ride with
them. They flanked him and rode quickly toward the
main lodges.

Spur looked for the white girl but did not see her.
There were many other normal activities. He paused
where three Indian women were cutting up buffalo
meat into thin slices and hanging it on racks in the
sun to dry. The strips were a foot long and two
inches wide, but no more than a quarter of an inch
thick.

He pointed at the meat and then at the escort.
Spur signed: HOW MANY DAYS TO DRY
MEAT?

The brave understood but he shrugged. Then Spur
realized that he had asked a question about squaw
work. A brave was not interested in such matters.
Women ran the camp, even put up and took down
the cumbersome tipis and transported them when
the people moved.

The braves had to be ready at all times to defend
the camp, the band, the family. That was their
responsibility. That was why the braves never
carried anything when they moved, and never did
small tasks around the camp. Spur hoped he had not
offended the brave.

They stopped a few yards later at the same big
tipi he had on his first trip, and Spur dismounted as
he did before, leaving his rifle in its boot, and
removing his "short bang, bang," and placing it in
his saddle bag. He had no thought that it might be
stolen.

When Spur had put the gun away, Chief Many
Winters came out of his tipi. Spur made the sign of
friend, which the old Indian repeated.

WALK WITH ME, the chief signed. Spur nodded
and they left the escort and horses and walked

through the camp of many lodges. Spur watched but he did not see the white girl.

They came near an old man making a new bow, and Spur pointed and signed to the chief. HOW IS BOW MADE? The chief nodded and led him to the old man. The Indian was probably over sixty. He had twisted legs and feet, but his torso was strong and his arms like steel bands.

The chief said something to him and he looked at Spur in surprise. Spur figured he was the first roundeye the old man had ever seen close up. He squinted for a minute and Spur smiled at him and gave him one of the mirrors. The old man glanced in it a moment, then nodded and slid it under his buffalo robe where he sat. He would give it to his beautiful daughter.

The chief spoke with the bow maker a moment, then signalled and Dog Piss came up behind them.

"Why would roundeye want to know about bows?" Dog Piss asked.

"So I'll know," Spur replied. The chief motioned sharply to Dog Piss who was to be interpreter.

The story came out slowly. The old Indian took a stick from a bunch of ten, twelve he had and placed it beside Spur's leg. He marked it where it came to Spur's waist.

"It is orangewood, and is best for bows," Dog Piss said. He was not enjoying his task. "Orangewood is best because it won't split when it dries. It grows even farther north than here and is hard to find."

He went on: "Young ash that's been left dead by a fire is good for a bow. Elm, cedar, willow, dogwood, even mulberry will work fine if you get winter wood so it won't split when dried.

"Trim the bark off the sticks and rub them with

buffalo fat. Then tie them in bundles of ten or twelve and hang them near the top of your lodge. The smoke will season the sticks and kill any worms in them.''

The old Indian showed on the piece he had how he had been shaping it, carving from the center outward. The center would be the grip.

''After carving the bow to the right shape, smooth and polish it with sandstone.''

The old Indian bow maker rubbed fat into the end of the bow he was working on and then held the end over the fire until it became very hot. Then quickly he held the hot end under his moccasin and bent the end into a graceful curve. The old Indian held the bow in that position for several minutes as it cooled.

'He's bending the bow so it will have a curve. When it cools the wood will stay in that shape. Hardest part is to make the curve the same on each end of the bow. The curve must be the same and many times the curve must be rubbed with fat and heated again and the curve changed until it is just right.''

Dog Piss looked at the chief who nodded.

They watched the bow maker smoothing the grip.

Dog Piss picked up the narration. ''The grip must be thick enough or the bow will kick back when you shoot it which can make the bow string burn your wrist. The ends of the bow should be as wide as the shooter's little finger. The bigger the man, the bigger and heavier the bow.''

They watched for a moment longer. It was obvious that Dog Piss was not pleased with his role. He looked at the chief again, and scowled, but continued.

''The bowstring is made from buffalo sinew that usually is about eighteen inches long. The bow maker splits off two pieces of it and soaks them in his mouth."

The old man spit out the sinew and rolled it between his palm and his bare thigh. Quickly he added a first to the end of the second and rolled it, then added a third until he had one long piece of the sinew of even diameter and three times the length of the bow.

This long piece was then doubled in thirds and twisted into a three-strand cord that he knotted on both ends so it wouldn't unravel. Then he tied it tightly between two stakes to keep it stretched as it dried.

Dog Piss picked up the end of the work. "In a day he will have a perfect, strong bowstring just the right length for this bow."

The old chief nodded and Dog Piss returned to where he had been, following six paces behind them.

A short time later they sat on a low bluff overlooking the Souris River. It was much smaller here than at Minot.

The old chief signed: YOU COME ABOUT THE RIFLES.

Spur signed, YES.

Chief Many Winters continued signing: WE DESTROY THEM. BUT USE PARTS, METAL FOR ARROW TIPS. WOOD FOR CARVING. ALL DESTROYED.

Spur nodded, HOW MANY LONG BANGS DESTROYED?

THIRTY-EIGHT.

Spur lifted his brows. The old chief nodded. Spur signed again.

CHIEF SPEAK TRUE. I AM PLEASED. PEACE BETWEEN OUR PEOPLE.

The chief reached out as the roundeyes did and

gripped hands. He was not sure why, but roundeyes always did it. They sat a moment watching the river, then the village of sixty lodges. Spur was satisfied that the chief had not allowed any of the rifles to be kept by his people. He was an honorable man.

But Spur had no idea how to raise the question of the small white girl. If he could see her again. That had not happened.

He watched the old chief. Then signed:

WHITE GIRL LIVE AMONG YOU.

YES, MAKES ME LAUGH, DEER KILLER'S DAUGHTER.

Spur plunged on. IS SHE SLAVE?

NO, MEMBER FAMILY. DEER KILLER HER FATHER.

Spur knew he was in a dangerous area. WAS MAKES ME LAUGH CAPTURED IN A RAID?

Chief Many Winters frowned, shifted his weight, and Dog Piss, sitting six paces behind them, looked angry.

YES. IT IS THE PEOPLE'S WAY.

IS MAKES ME LAUGH HAPPY?

The chief stood with difficulty, motioned to Spur to follow him and they walked down to the lodges, past ten or fifteen until they came to a tipi that had one side of pure white skins that had been dusted with age.

He called sharply and a moment later the white girl Spur had seen before came out the flap of the tipi. She looked at the chief and smiled, then saw Spur and she froze, ready to run like a startled fawn.

She looked about the same, wearing a knee-length dress of doeskin, and moccasins. Chief Many Winters said something softly to her and she relaxed. Then he signed to Spur: ASK IF SHE IS HAPPY.

Spur moved closer to the girl. Her blonde hair was still nearly white where it had been sun bleached so much, but now it was greased so it would not fly in the wind. Her eyes were soft blue, her face toasted to a light almond shade. She looked as healthy as a cub bear.

Spur spoke slowly. "Makes Me Laugh, are you happy here?"

She frowned, then looked at the chief. He nodded. She spoke slowly at first in the language of the people, but she stopped at a motion from the chief. She blinked, creased her forehead and began again.

"Yes, happy here. English I almost forget."

"What's your roundeye name?"

"Beth Kline."

"How long have you been here with the people?"

"Two winters."

"Where did you live before?"

"Live?"

"Your lodge, your real parents?"

"Live . . . Wisconsin, I think."

"Are you happy here?"

"Yes, my people. Deer Killer my father. I am their daughter. I have my own pony! I can scrape hides, makes clothes. Always Happy, my mother, is good to me."

"Would you like to go back to your family in Wisconsin?"

Makes Me Laugh turned and ran into the lodge.

Both men stood there watching the empty flap. Several minutes later she came out. An Indian woman. Always Happy, who was short and heavy, came with her. Makes Me Laugh looked at her Indian mother. The woman nodded.

"No family left," the girl said.

Spur took a deep beath. "They are all dead?"

She nodded.

"Do you wish to stay here, live with the people?"

"Yes, forever and forever."

"You may, then, Makes Me Laugh. Tell the chief I have no reason to take you away."

She smiled and chattered with the chief for a moment. The old headman smiled.

"Now, can you show me the camp? Ask Chief Many Winters if you may."

She spoke again. The old man nodded at her mother, who answered quickly.

"Yes, I may. It is good to speak English again. What do you want to see?"

"Everything. And be sure to remember and practice your English so you can speak for your new people with the roundeyes. There will be more need for interpreters in the years to come. Can you read and write? You should learn. That way you can help your people more."

"I would like to learn."

"I'll send you some reading books."

They spent the rest of the morning going through the camp. She showed him her pony, Swift Wind, took him to the field where they played a game called stick, something like field hockey. They saw the old men sitting in front of their lodges. He ate the noon meal with them. She told him it was dried buffalo meat dipped in honey. A treat just for him.

Soon it was too late to leave and he agreed to stay the night. Makes Me Laugh asked her mother if he could stay in their lodge. She agreed. Spur found his horse and brought out the mirrors, three of them. One for the blonde girl, one for her mother, and one for another woman, a widow, who lived in their lodge. The ladies stared at their reflections, giggled and laughed. Makes Me Laugh hurried off to show her treasure to a small friend.

Spur sat by the fire in the center of the lodge and talked in sign language with Deer Killer. He was a brave without children, and he had three women to hunt for. It was hard for him. He said the camp would be moving again soon. They shifted from place to place so they did not use up all the grass for their horses, and so the buffalo were not too far from them.

There was much work to do before winter when they needed several rawhide boxes filled with the delicious pemmican for their winter's food.

They talked late into the evening, and when Spur saw his hosts' eyes slip closed the second time, he signed that he was sleepy. They gave him a beautiful fox robe with double hair on it that would be soft and warm for him to sleep under.

The next morning he woke early but stayed in the smoky lodge until it was bustling with activity. He asked to see the chief again, and signed briefly with him to take care of Makes Me Laugh. He told the old chief the girl was smart and should be his voice with the roundeyes. He could always trust Makes Me Laugh, he could not always trust Dog Piss.

The chief nodded in agreement.

"I want to ride with you as far as the black thornberries," Makes Me Laugh said shyly. "Would it be all right?"

"Of course."

She squealed in delight and ran to bring her pony. She rode bareback, her soft doeskin dress billowing around her.

The blackberry patch was two miles down river, and Spur saw two braves riding a hundred yards behind them. At the patch of berries they got down and ate a few, then she ran up to him and gave him a hug and kissed his cheek.

"Grow straight and tall, Makes Me Laugh, and help your new people. Life will be harder and harder for them."

"I'll try," Makes Me Laugh said. For a moment he thought she wanted to come with him, then she turned, ran and vaulted on her pony and shrieked an Indian cry as she raced back toward the village.

Spur watched her go, held up his hand in a final wave and turned downstream.

He had a long ride ahead of him, and then the final tangle of the Tom Renshew case to resolve.

For another moment he thought of the small girl, Beth Kline, now known as Makes Me Laugh. She would do fine with the people, the Indian people.

He rode away quickly, anxious to get back to Minot.

17

Spur McCoy rode on toward Minot. He had taken his time coming back, even waded in the shallows of the Souris River once when the sun became hot. It felt good to slow down for a moment and smell the wild flowers.

Five miles out of Minot, he came to the turnoff where he could go west to the Renshew ranch. He kicked his pony that way. It was worth a try. If Wolf Vincent was still there it could work.

He stopped at the big ranch house. There were no guards out. When he knocked at the door a middle-aged woman answered.

"Ma'am, I'm hunting Wolf Vincent. I'm told he works here."

She scowled, nodded. "Out in the bunkhouse. Should be out with the crew working, but he hurt his arms."

"Thank you, ma'am, nothing important, just need to see him for a minute."

"Help yourself."

Spur rode over to the bunkhouse and slid down,

tied his horse and went inside. It was like most
bunkhouses. Cheaply made, designed to sleep ten or
twenty men with no privacy, and no room to do
much else. This one had a fireplace and two easy
chairs in the front end. In one of them sat a man
with a bandaged right arm.

"Vincent?" Spur asked.

The man began to claw for a six-gun, but Spur
beat him with the draw and Vincent's left hand fell
to his side.

"Vincent, Wolf Vincent?"

The man nodded.

"Relax. I'm not here to hurt you. I have a favor I
want to ask of you." Spur holstered his iron.

"You joking? You're the guy who busted up the
boss. You're that government man."

"Right. And we bleed just like anybody else. You
know your way around the Yanktonai tribe, right?"

"Yeah, that's not a Federal crime."

"Good." Spur tossed him a twenty dollar gold
piece. "That's yours. What I need is a package
delivered to Makes Me Laugh in Deer Killer's lodge,
every four or five months, say twice a year. Can you
do that?"

Wolf laughed dryly. "Long as it ain't rifles."

"I've just come from talking with Chief Many
Winters. I've talked with Makes Me Laugh, the
white girl up there. She needs to learn to read and
write so she can help her adopted parents. So she
can be an interpreter for them."

"Might help a little for a while. The Indian's time
is running out. The Indians are doomed."

"Will you help me help her?"

Wolf took a deep breath. "You don't wonder how I
hurt my arm?"

Spur grinned. "Probably a fifty-six caliber rifle

round. Could have come from my Spencer. We won't worry about that if you do me this favor."

Wolf sat up straighter. "Just deliver the books, tablets, pencils. That kind of thing?"

"Yes, twice a year. Pick them up from Virginia at Frances's stitchery shop. Take them up and bring back a gift from Makes Me Laugh to Virginia. Easy."

"I get paid?"

"You get twenty dollars for every trip."

Wolf stood up and held out his hand. "Yes, I can do it. I'll keep track of Many Winters' band when they move." He hesitated. "You think this might help my tribe?"

"I hope so, Wolf. I truly hope so. You call on Virginia McCoy at the dress shop next week. She'll have a package ready."

They shook hands again, and Spur went out and stepped up into his saddle.

It was such a small thing, he had no idea why he felt so damn good.

He rode a little faster then, and came into Minot just after eight o'clock. He stopped first at the Livery, then at the sheriff's office. The top man was still there.

When Spur came into the sheriff's private office, one of the clerks from the District Attorney's office was there taking down a letter on a pad of paper. Sheriff Sweet looked up and grinned.

"Things been popping around here since you left, McCoy. The very next day after you left, Judge Robinson came to town straight from Bismarck. He claimed he'd been sent up special. Ha! I told him I'd challenge him as a partial jurist since he'd been on Tom Renshew's payroll for the past fifteen years.

"Old geezer almost had a heart attack. I sent him

packing on the afternoon stage. Also sent another letter demanding an impartial circuit court judge. Yes sir, things are popping around here."

"How is the prisoner?"

"He's fine. Yells a lot. Wants special privileges, which he don't get. Two meals a day and a piss pot. More than he's got coming, my way of thinking."

"How long were you on the Renshew payroll, Sheriff Sweet?"

"Never was. No sir. I made that plain. But I admit I was afraid of him. The man scared the shit out of me, you want the plain truth. But now, I don't scare."

"Everything else on schedule? The District Attorney filed the proper papers?"

"Right, filed with the county, all legal. We're just waiting for a judge."

"Good, I've had a long ride."

"Where you going? All the excitement is around here. Has been for three days."

"Enjoy it," Spur said. "I'm getting a big steak dinner, then a hot bath and twenty-four hours of sleep."

"I'll call you if anything exciting happens."

Spur made it to his room, dumped his gear, washed up and hit the dining room just before it closed. Yes, they still had a big steak, medium rare. They would bring it with everything they had left over.

As Spur waited for his food he had a cold beer and when he turned around, Virginia came in. She slid to a seat across his table for two and smiled.

"My spies told me you were back. What happened?"

"Hello, how are you, I'm fine, thanks, you're looking great and I hope your family is well. Now that we have that out of the way, it happened. Sounds like you had some excitement here."

"The judge? Yeah. I told Sweet to boot his bottom out of town. Now, did you find the little white girl?"

Spur told her the story. When he finished, Virginia touched a tear off her cheek.

"Poor little tyke. Family all slaughtered while she watched, then she probably was tied on a horse and raced across the country. She might have been traded three or four times before she came to this tribe."

"Her parents seem genuinely fond of her. They have no other kids, so they really need her. You should have seen her ride! No saddle, astride. She could probably ride without using her hands better than I can using both of mine. She's bright, and quick and smart. I told her to keep using her English."

"Good, aren't you about done with your dinner?"

"It hasn't come yet. A good steak takes a half hour to cook it right so it isn't burned on the outside."

"I'll have some coffee." She looked at his bottle of beer. "How did you get beer? They don't serve beer in the dining room!"

Spur laughed. "I must have asked for it with such a mean face they thought they better humor me. Anyway the dining room is closed."

"I missed you."

"That you know you'll have to get used to. Did I tell you that Frances likes you. She tells me that she'll have you married in three years."

Virginia laughed. "Nobody would have me around this town."

"She didn't say you'd be married in this town. Don't underestimate Frances. She used to be a slave."

His steak arrived with seven side dishes. The waitress grinned as she put them down.

"I went around emptying out every pot of vegetables we had back there. Hope the steak is right."

Spur thanked her and dug in. Virginia sneaked a bite off the thin part of the steak, then had another one. They were the only ones left in the dining room.

"I hope you plan on staying for the trial," Virginia said. "It could be any day now."

"Probably not. The defense will ask for more time to prepare, they always do."

"Not Renshew. He's determined to be found guilty of murder so he can hang."

"Couldn't happen to a more deserving guy."

Twenty minutes later they went up to Spur's room and he ordered the portable bath tub brought in and four buckets of hot water.

"A bath for two?" she asked.

"Two or three, you have a friend?" She hit him on the shoulder.

"Things are going right at the dress shop?"

"Yes. I'm going to be a seamstress in just no time. I've always liked to sew, and Frances says I have a flair for stitchery. I'm trying to design some things of my own."

She walked up to him where he stood by the bed and reached up as high as she could, then pulled his face down and kissed him. She sighed softly.

"I've been waiting days to do that again."

"You should have attacked me on the street." He grinned. "Oh, I have a job for you." He pulled out his wallet and took from it a hundred dollar bill. He gave it to her.

"Honey, I stopped doing it for money, remember?"

"Not this you haven't." He explained to her about the school books he wanted for Makes Me Laugh. He told her that Wolf Vincent would deliver them to the little white girl every six months.

"Put together whatever you think she should have. A first grade reader to start, a tablet, some pencils, maybe some crayons. She'll need to learn to read and write all by herself."

Virginia's eyes sparkled. "Yes, yes! That will be easy. I'll get books from the school. They must have some old ones. What's all the money for?"

"Wolf gets twenty dollars for each trip. When you run out of money, send a notice to me at the St. Louis office. I'll replenish your supply."

"Could I go up and visit her?"

Spur laughed. "Not unless you want to stay as a slave or a white squaw. These are reasonable Indians, but you would be so luscious a morsel you'd never get away."

The bathtub and water came, and they splashed in it and tested it.

"We have our party before, or after the bath?" Virginia asked.

"After and maybe during, who knows?"

They slid out of their clothes and tested the water. It was still hot.

Virginia caught his hand and led him to the bed and pushed Spur down on it.

"Maybe we should wait just a minute for the water to cool down," she said. She spread Spur out on the bed on his back and then slithered over him until her breasts brushed his lips.

"You could be right," Spur said. He was wondering what his next assignment would be. He could remember everything now. He would have to ride the stage to Bismarck to find a telegraph.

No matter, there would be a new job waiting for

him whenever he checked in. He really should stay another day or two, or three or four to be sure that the trial got started right. Yes, he was sure of it.

"Are you sure of it?" Spur asked the creature who had captured him.

"Sure of what?" she asked, dropping one full breast directly into his mouth.

For the moment Spur couldn't reply.

"What the hell," he thought. "Two or three more days of rest and recuperation would be fine."